BRUSHSTROKES OF LOVE

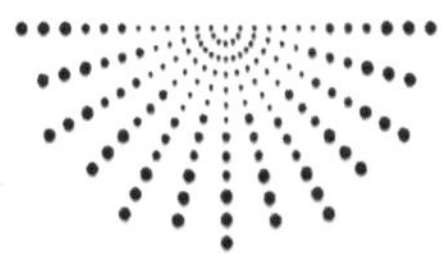

ALISON JOY

DRAGONFLY BLUE ENTERPRISES

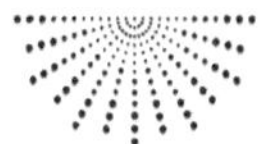

*M*atisse stared at the ring on her left hand, almost convinced she had imagined the whole thing. The buzz of noise around them died down as the other diners returned to their meals.

Across the intimate restaurant table, Jonno sat with a self-satisfied gleam in his eyes and a glass of wine in his hand. Picking up her own glass, she raised it towards his as they saluted the next chapter of their lives.

Finding love hadn't been part of the plan when she'd first arrived in Bali ten months earlier for a change of scenery. The actual plan had been to find some inspiration to paint. She had led a relatively quiet existence until Jonno and his laidback larrikin charm invaded her world. And now here she was—totally smitten with a wonderful man, a fellow Aussie.

The surfing holiday he had planned with his uni mates had long ended. He had waved them all off, moved in with her, and was working in the bar of this very restaurant, and surfing in his spare time. Idyllic, but the sacrifice he was making for love wasn't lost on her. There had been some difficulties with his family, but she was hopeful that was in the past.

She wished she could be as unconcerned as Jonno seemed to

be. Pushing doubt aside, she focused on her now-fiancé. That grin of his got her. Every. Single. Time. Not to mention those deep blue eyes that pulled her in.

After dinner, they went to the nearby beach for a stroll along the moonlit sand before heading home. As she pulled her helmet from the scooter, he reached for yet another kiss. She settled the helmet on her head and adjusted the fit.

Climbing on behind Jonno, she tousled his sun-bleached hair then put her arms around him as he started the scooter. Flicking the kickstand up, he took off, fishtailing slightly on the loose gravel of the carpark. Grabbing him tighter as they lurched, she resettled herself, squeezing her knees firmly.

Jonno expertly turned the scooter across the road when there was a break in the traffic, and joined the stream of vehicles. Even at this hour, the road was busy, and Jonno weaved in and out of the traffic. She wasn't a fan of the scooter. Especially at night. There were enough stories of tourists getting seriously hurt or worse.

She tried to consciously relax, taking a couple of deeper breaths. His white cotton shirt had come loose from his pants on one side and was flapping in the wind. Jonno was saying something to her, but she couldn't hear him as he reached back and patted her knee. She pushed his elbow so he would get the hint and grab the handlebar again. Just as they approached the major intersection, her world suddenly went black.

It stayed that way for a very long time.

CHAPTER ONE

"Are you sure this is a good idea, Matisse? This place has no electricity or running water."

"It'll be fine, Max," she reassured him. "No different to camping, but with a cabin instead of a tent."

"Six months is a bit more than a camping trip."

She shook her head as Max looked on with a mixture of affection and concern. Matisse took the last of the pile of canvases from him and strained to shove them into the over-stuffed van, grunting to slam the door shut. Avoiding his gaze, she pulled the yellow bandanna from around her hair and retied it. She was glad she had already said farewell to his wife a few days earlier when Dee had gone to stay with her ill sister. There's no way she'd cope with both of them hovering around her.

She tugged at the sleeve of her blouse. He had a right to be concerned, after all she'd put him and Deidre through in the twenty months since the accident. She'd never be able to grasp how hard it must have been for him to fly in from Sydney to sit by her broken body in the hospital, not knowing if he'd take her home alive.

Trying not to dwell on the accident wasn't easy. At times, it was emotionally overwhelming. Like now. She busied herself rolling the leg hems of her denim overalls to give herself a chance to pull in a few inconspicuous deep breaths. Surely she'd cried enough. For herself. For Jonno. Of course, she'd been planning to tell Max and Dee about her engagement. They had met Jonno earlier. Surely they would've been happy for her?

But ... she needed to try and find her way again. After all the rehab, it had been months before she could bring herself to paint again, but she was ever so slowly clawing her way out of the darkness she had tumbled into. Matisse tightened the laces on her shoes. Painting was so intrinsically interwoven with the very essence of who she was. It was as if the creative light had been snuffed out on the road in Bali. She needed to try to find herself again. Getting away from her spot in Max and Dee's Bondi apartment was necessary for her. For all of them. She could never repay them for their faith and support over the years, especially since her mother's death. Standing up, she gave her mentor a quick hug and climbed into the van.

"Bye, Max, give my love to Dee."

MATISSE INTENDED to meander down to the Victorian town of Apollo Bay via the coast in about ten days, stopping here and there at whim. At Kiama, she joined the people lined up on the viewing platform waiting for the plumes of water to shoot up from the famous blowhole. She wasn't disappointed, thanks to a south-east wind that helped push the water high into the cloudless blue sky. Putting Max and Deidre's gift of a camera to good use, she snapped away at the landscape for future painting inspiration.

By the time she rolled into the seaside village of Hyams Beach on the shores of Jervis Bay late on the first day, she was tired. She had kept busy for weeks—organising her trip, packing everything. Upbeat music had distracted her in her van as she drove. But when she climbed between the cool sheets of the hotel bed that night, she was utterly alone for the first time ... since Jonno came into her life. Even after the accident she hadn't been alone—between doctors and nurses and then Max and Dee.

The crashing of the waves reached her in the hotel room, reminding her of her home in Bali—and Jonno. Her body ached for his caress, his voice—the smell of him after he'd just come back from a surf. The way he would steal into bed and enfold her in his arms after his shift at the local bar.

After all this time, Jonno was never far from her thoughts. Sometimes she could go an hour or two without thinking of him, but more often than not he was hovering in the background—just out of her mind's line of sight. Sometimes he would sneak into her thoughts and she would smile, remembering something he'd said or done. Other times, he would slam right into her consciousness and the pain would make it hard for her to breathe, let alone function with any degree of normality. Every day was different. No, more than that, every hour was able to conjure up the whole gamut of emotions. It was draining physically as well as mentally.

Now, in the darkness of the hotel room, huge gut-wrenching sobs wracked her body. All she could do was lie in the dark until exhaustion overtook her and she slept.

Early in the morning, emotionally spent, she walked down a side street to the beach to watch the sunrise. Curled up with her knees against her chest, she waited as the morning colours chased each other across the new day. Jervis Bay supposedly had the whitest sand anywhere in the world, and looking around at the expanse, she didn't doubt it. Even the white sand of Bali's Pasir Putih Beach couldn't compare.

One of the touristy things to do in Jervis Bay was a dolphin cruise—so she spent a couple of hours checking out the bottlenose dolphins with other visitors. Not in the frame of mind to socialise, she shielded herself behind her camera. As usual, her thoughts scattered. *What would Jonno have thought of the dolphins? Of Jervis Bay? Had he been here? Did he ever mention it?*

Disembarking from the boat she headed back along the footpath, only to be blindsided by a guy—just walking with his family along the foreshore—who looked so much like Jonno, she started to tear up. She fought to catch her breath and dashed for the safety of the van, slamming the door shut. Quickly backing out of the carpark, she turned on to the highway, but had to pull off to the side. That guy. He had a family—something she would never have with Jonno. Wallowing in self-pity, 'it took her a good while before she could pull herself together enough to continue to drive.

DAYS LATER, and after more than a thousand kilometres of road, Matisse drove under the wooden memorial arch that stretched across the highway, announcing the start of the Great Ocean Road. The two hundred and forty-three-kilometre road, built by returned servicemen, ran from the town of Torquay to Port Fairy. She was grateful for every twist and turn in the bitumen that forced her to concentrate on the task at hand and not dwell on Jonno.

Stopping often, wherever there was a lookout, she took photos and enjoyed the spectacular coastal scenery. The clifftop views were eye-poppingly breathtaking. *Is that even a phrase? Well, if not, it should be.* Against a backdrop of clear azure sky, vegetation flowed down the cliff face like green lava, only to be halted by charcoal rock formations that crowded its base and were engulfed by the swirling white froth of the Southern Ocean.

It was easy to lose track of time. When Matisse finally arrived in the little town of Apollo Bay, she was too late to pick up the keys for her cabin. Instead, she made a reconnaissance of the town so she could get going early in the morning and buy supplies before heading out.

She touched base with Max. There would be no phone reception where she was heading, and she knew that worried him.

~

THE RECEPTIONIST at the real estate office handed over a copy of all the signed paperwork, along with a set of keys. "Take the Cape Otway turn-off just out of town," she told Matisse, reading from a sheet of paper in front of her in a mid-western American accent, hardly making eye contact. "The entrance to the property is about two-thirds of the way in along the road. It isn't easy to find. There's a yellow reflective marker on a tree by the side of the road—but blink and you'll miss it. If you get to the lighthouse, then you've gone too far. This key," she told Matisse, fingering one in the bunch, "is for the gate. It's a back way into the property. And this is for the cabin door. I'm not sure about these others, but I guess you'll figure it out. Make sure you shut and padlock the gate behind yourself."

"Thanks."

"Oh and watch out for the koalas. Or rather, the cars stopping suddenly to take photos of the koalas. That area has a large population of them—unsustainable. You'll see some of the manna gums there have been stripped bare."

~

MATISSE DOUBLE-CHECKED EVERYTHING. She had no idea how her food supply would pan out, but at least town would be only half an hour away. Pulling herself into the van with a sigh, she put it into gear. The vehicle wasn't brand-new, and she was glad Max had insisted on having it checked over mechanically before she set off.

Soon after she turned off the Great Ocean Road, she slowed at the sight of lots of cars parked by the side of the road. People wandered along the shoulder on both sides. It looked like dozens of photos were being taken. A mother and father pointed up into a tree as their three excited young children looked on. She caught a glimpse of grey bumps in a couple of the manna gums closest to the road. Matisse decided to return another time to take her own koala photographs.

In a short space of driving time, the green of the gum trees gave way to bare branches that reached across to each other from either side. Once upon a time it would have been a beautiful canopy of green, but now the branches, stripped bare of their foliage by koalas, stood starkly against the blue of the sky. The still-green undergrowth around the base of the manna gums gave the scene an otherworldly feel.

When the red-lettered "Welcome to Cape Otway" sign came into view, she realised she had driven too far. Blowing out a breath of frustration she looked for a place to swing the van around. Retracing her route, a line-up of cars quickly formed behind her as she drove slowly, so she didn't miss the entry.

Finally, she spotted the roadside marker and turned across the road. The track was narrow. So was the gate. Barely wide enough for her vehicle to get through. Making sure to swing the rusty metal gate closed behind her, Matisse wrapped the thick chain back around and snapped the padlock into place. All she had to do now was follow the deeply rutted track. Maybe a four-wheel drive would have been a better choice of vehicle.

As THE TALL trees closed in, dwarfing her, it became noticeably cooler. She emerged into a large clearing and saw a cabin just ahead. Pulling up in front, Matisse switched off the ignition and leaned her arms across the steering wheel, taking in her new abode.

It was a rustic slab hut like the ones she'd only seen in calendars or pictorial books. The roof was a patchwork of brown, rusted sections over the light-coloured galvanised metal. Rough timber planks, weathered to a soft grey, stood vertically in sections to form the walls. Rails, each fashioned from a single tree branch, ran horizontally the length of the front veranda. Either side of the door was a four-pane window. The corner of one was taped across an obvious crack. The window on the opposite side of the door was missing a pane altogether, with a piece of timber fastened across the gap from the inside.

A lean-to of sorts attached to the right of the cabin looked like it should accommodate the van. Just. She took the three steps up to the front veranda and cautiously stepped over the damaged timber sections to the solid, rough-hewn door.

The key she pushed into the lock didn't turn. Certain it was the one the real estate worker had identified as the front door key, she wriggled and shook the battered black doorknob, then tried the other keys in the small bunch, worried she might have to trek back to the real estate office. After a few frustrating minutes, a key finally turned in the lock. Matisse held her breath as she leaned on the door to push it open with her shoulder.

Okay, so she hadn't really known what to expect. She knew it was an old logger's cabin. "Old" being the operative word. It was probably not much bigger than a double garage. As she stepped across the threshold, she noticed several floorboards had been replaced. On the left-hand side, two small rooms had been created. There were no doors on them. Maybe space for a double bed in the first one but little else. The second room was even smaller—that was where she decided to store her art gear.

Her qualms about the state of the cabin disappeared as soon as she spotted the window. On the back wall, a newly added picture window framed the trees and surrounding greenery perfectly. She would set up her easel next to it. On the right side of the cabin were two very narrow rooms. One might be a kitchenette down the track—for now there was a narrow timber bench along the side wall. Nothing else. The other room might eventually house a tiny bathroom.

It seemed odd that the owner had rented the cabin out in this partly renovated state, but Matisse reasoned that maybe he or she had run out of money and needed to recoup some costs before continuing. The place could do with a good sweep and mop. *You'd think some cleaning could've been done before it was let out.*

Matisse struggled to get the back door open, and stepped out onto another veranda, in more need of repair than the one at the front. It looked like most of the boards needed replacing. She picked her way along its length. The horizontal, waist-high rail moved under her hand as she touched it, and she made a mental note never to lean on it. Stepping gingerly over the rotten boards she stood at the top step.

There was a water tank in a precarious position to the right of the cabin, in front of the lean-to—well, you couldn't really call it a carport. A small building housing a composting toilet was a few more steps beyond that. Stepping down over a broken stair tread, she realised she could hear the water from the creek and walked about ten metres to its edge.

She breathed in deeply. The air was different here—even to the air in Apollo Bay. Maybe it was the crispness coming from the Southern Ocean nearby, mixed with the scent of the surrounding trees. After a few breaths, she could feel herself starting to relax. The Cape was already starting to weave some magic on her wounded soul. To her left was a perfect spot where she could sit on rocks and listen to the water, watching as it cascaded down the creek. As much as she wanted to follow its path, for now she had to unpack.

Emptying the van seemed to take forever. She hauled bedding and clothes into the first room. Art gear into the second. A camping table and chairs for the main area. A picnic set, gas cooker and a box of pots and utensils for the narrower kitchen area. The food was in large clear plastic boxes with snap lock lids, and she'd topped up her gas bottle in town to run the camping fridge.

It was getting late by the time she pulled the van in around the side. She just managed to squeeze out between the door and the lean-to wall. Matisse set up her camp stretcher with its bedding and dug around to find the portable lighting. Pulling one of the camping chairs out to the back veranda, she tested the timber before she sat, grateful for a cuppa from the thermos she had filled before leaving the hotel. A couple of pieces of fruit and a leftover bread roll spread with Vegemite served as dinner.

Listening to the unfamiliar noises as night settled over the cabin, Matisse tossed and turned, trying to find a comfortable position on the camp stretcher. Had she made a good decision? Maybe she should have picked one of the little beach-side towns like Batemans Bay or Merimbula, so she was within striking distance of Sydney and, more importantly, to Max and Dee. She had needed to get away but maybe this was too far, too soon.

Damn but this bed was uncomfortable. She wriggled around and bashed at her pillow. Getting decent sleep was difficult enough without adding the camp stretcher to the mix. It didn't bode well.

Suck it up, princess. You just need to find the rhythm of your new surroundings.

Two days later, Matisse ventured back into town at lunchtime. The main street was crowded with Chinese tourists. Apparently, Apollo Bay was a lunch stop for some of the tour companies. There were several coaches parked in the side streets. Maybe it would be better coming into town later in the day when it wasn't so busy. Dodging dawdling tourists, she eventually found the post office, then contacted Max to arrange for her mail to be forwarded while making light of her accommodation.

As she drove back out to the Cape, she figured it might work to make a trip back into town maybe every ten days to replenish supplies, if she could manage that long. Staying in town overnight would mean a decent shower and real bed to enjoy.

Back at the cabin, she unrolled her new calico drop cloth and spread it out on the floor, folding the ends to fit the space. A small card table held her main paints and brushes, with the overflow in a plastic tub underneath. A large box of notebooks and papers was shoved into a corner of the room. Against one of the walls in the smaller room, she stacked a pile of new canvases of varying sizes, then spread a number of unfinished ones along the adjacent side. No doubt the arrangement would change once her creative rhythm evolved.

Hands on hips, she surveyed her new home, but she couldn't help the frisson of doubt creeping through her mind. Was she doing the right thing? Would she even be able to cope with the quiet and isolation? And how safe was it here, really?

The negative self-talk would defeat her if she let it—and she wasn't about to let that happen.

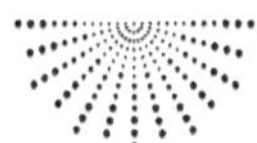

CHAPTER TWO

Jake loaded tools into the back of his dark blue Ford Ranger four-wheel drive ute. Despite arriving home late last night from a business trip to Melbourne, he had already made an early morning drive to his parents' home and back to collect his canine friend, then he'd taken a conference call that took longer than he anticipated. Now he was keen to get back down to the old cabin. He added a sleeping bag and esky of food, figuring he'd be staying overnight.

Jake had spent a lot of time at the tiny cabin over the years. Realistically, he should have knocked it down, but he had decided to preserve the old building, keeping any renovations in sympathy with the original structure. The wood he needed for repairs was sourced from fallen logs on the property. A neighbour with a bush mill helped him prepare and dress the timber.

The family of his best friend growing up had originally owned the surrounding land. When the property came on the market three years ago, he'd jumped at the chance to buy it, pleased to be able to establish a home base for himself.

A whistle summoned his three-year-old black Labrador, Charlie, who bounded out from where he'd been sniffing trees, and jumped into the back of the ute, happy to be with his master again. Jake backed out onto the wide concrete apron, then turned up the steep drive past his cement-rendered house. Charlie trotted back and forth from one side of the tray to the other as they passed the distinctive navy and red colours of the Davis Air helicopter on its concrete pad.

The track down to the other end of his property was well-worn—a little rutted in places, but he didn't mind. Leaning his elbow out the open window, he enjoyed the breeze. So fresh and clean after the city confines. Charlie barked in appreciation as they drove, poking his head around the side near his master's window.

When he came in sight of the cabin, Jacob saw a white van parked in the lean-to. "Backpackers again." He scowled. At least the van wasn't one of those crudely graffitied versions he'd seen lately. He detested those, surprised their crass signage was even allowed on the roads.

In the past he'd had trouble with unauthorised entry to the property, even though the access gate was securely locked. As he slowed to a stop alongside the lean-to, Charlie jumped down and took off towards the creek, probably on the scent of a rabbit.

No one seemed to be about. He checked through the cabin window. There was a fair bit of gear. Someone certainly seemed to have settled in. He was not looking forward to yet another confrontation.

MATISSE WAS on her way back from a walk along the creek when a black Lab. came bounding up out of nowhere, determined to make friends.

"Hello, boy. Where did you come from?" Reaching down she read his collar tag. "Hey, Charlie, where's your owner?" Charlie just sat and lapped up the attention as she patted his head and ran her hand along his back all the way to his tail.

A loud whistle startled her, and she looked up as Charlie

took off. Charlie's owner? Well, he was tall and well-built, dressed in faded jeans, worn boots and a red shirt with sleeves rolled up. The black Akubra he was wearing obscured his face until he got closer. With each stride he took in her direction, she felt a geyser of nervous energy surge inside her.

His eyes were dark and piercing as they regarded her. "You're trespassing on private property."

"I'm not, actually."

He seemed not to have heard her. "You backpackers have some nerve, thinking you can just break into a place and make yourself at home."

"But I didn't break in, and I'm not a backpacker—"

"How did you find out about the cabin? Is there some sort of backpacker grapevine that passes on details of places to stay?"

She tried to tell him about the real estate agent in town, but he just kept talking.

"What did you use to get in? The gate is chained and padlocked. Did you use bolt cutters? I've a good mind to call the police."

"No, I have a key." That finally got his attention.

"Pardon?" he looked at her in disbelief.

"I have a key. I'm renting the cabin." She indicated the building behind him with an air of exasperation.

"What? It's not available to rent."

"Sorry, that's not what the real estate agent told me. Are you the manager?"

He just nodded.

"I have paperwork. I'll go and get it." She walked around him and went inside.

JAKE STOOD WAITING, arms folded, one foot resting on the bottom step. He expected to have seen a partner of some sort by now, but she appeared to be on her own. Where on earth had she come from and why was she even here on his property—practically in the middle of nowhere?

Jake had been taken aback to see the woman patting his dog. When she walked over, he thought maybe there was a bit of a limp in her gait. He couldn't help but check out her slim figure in faded, ripped, cut-off denim jeans and battered cream sneakers. She was wearing a hippie-type cream blouse with embroidery around the neckline. Her long, dark blonde hair was pulled back into a ponytail. As she got closer, he had been all at once transfixed by her dark green eyes—it would be so easy to get lost in them. Then her scent hit him. What was it? Coconut and ... frangipani? It reminded him of Fiji. She was entirely too good to be true. Gorgeous. Surely, he had imagined her?

His head snapped up as he heard her clear her throat. How long had she been trying to get his attention? Staying a couple of steps above him so he would have to look up, she thrust a sheaf of papers at him and shoved her paint-splattered hands into her back pockets, watching as he shuffled the papers. He pretended to take his time reading the paperwork as if he was studying every line. The truth was, she had unsettled him, and he was trying to regain his composure.

"This says Mat Reynolds."

"Yeah, that's me."

"Do you have some ID?" Okay, so it was a calculated move on his part to find out some more information. She disappeared inside again and came back offering her New South Wales driver's licence. He glanced at it.

Matisse Elizabeth Reynolds. He looked at her date of birth and did the math: thirty-two. There was also a Bondi address in Sydney. As he handed the card back her long fingers brushed his, sending a jolt through him. He was almost mesmerised as his gaze followed the rings on her fingers while she brushed a wisp of hair back into place, bracelets on her wrists jangling. Maybe she'd just come back from a Bali holiday—that was the kind of vibe she had going on.

"There seems to have been a mistake," he told her. "As you can tell, this place needs more work done on it before it can be rented. It won't be ready for another couple of months."

"I've just signed a six-month lease," she told him, gesturing to the paperwork.

He shrugged. "I'm not sure how it happened, but the cabin should not have been rented out."

"But I have a signed agreement." Her green eyes flashed indignantly.

"I'm sorry. I'll make sure you get your money back."

She put a hand on his arm, seemingly burning him in the process. He looked at her hand, not her eyes. "Please," she begged, "I need to get away for a bit and this spot is perfect. I knew what I was getting into when I signed up ... I'm prepared to pay you more ..."

Jake's mind scrolled through all the possibilities why she might be keen to stay in a place without amenities or phone reception. Rich girl running away from home, in trouble with the law, jilted lover—or worse, domestic violence.

He looked up at her.

Big mistake.

Those eyes!

The next thing, Jake was walking back to his ute, having agreed to let her stay. He still wasn't quite sure how that happened.

Then he remembered he'd gone to the cabin to do some work. Sighing, he backtracked.

She was sitting on the top step, leaning forward with her forearms resting on her legs, her fingers entwined, seemingly miles away. He could have just left again, and she wouldn't have noticed, but, in all honesty, she intrigued him, and he wanted to hang around.

~

MATISSE TOOK herself off to the creek with a camping chair and the latest mystery novel by her favourite author. The manager had come back and asked to do some repair work on the veranda. He had introduced himself as Jake. Nothing else was forthcoming. Going down by the creek was her attempt to put some distance between them. As if the dark-chocolate-brown eyes, designer stubble and rich voice weren't enough, as soon as her fingers had accidentally brushed his, he started messing with her equilibrium. That hadn't happened before. Not even with Jonno.

Remembering Jonno started the tears pricking at her eyes. But she found herself glancing over often to watch Jake work. Couldn't help herself. There was something about him that affected her. She couldn't identify what it was exactly. The day had warmed up, so he had discarded his overshirt, hanging it over the side mirror of his ute while he worked.

How can a white t-shirt look so good? she mused. *What was that corny expression? Sun's out, guns out?* Physical work looked good on him. Actually, any sort of work would look good on him. The waves of confidence rolling off him were evident from where she sat.

CHARLIE HAD GONE to sit by the chair at the creek. Jake could see she was absent-mindedly scratching the dog on the head as she read. Charlie was clearly besotted. He turned back to the job at hand, but kept looking up to check on Charlie—or so he kept telling himself. He didn't know what it was about her. Some unidentifiable quality. Aura? Maybe because she was a creative and he hadn't ever had much to do with artists. Thoughts kept rattling around his head as he tried to work. Several rotting boards on the veranda needed to be replaced. Ordinarily it shouldn't take him long to complete the job, but Jake's plan was to work at a slower pace and try to figure out his next move.

~

IF HE'D ASKED her about the book she was reading, Matisse wouldn't have been able to tell him anything about it. "I'm just stopping for some lunch," he told her as he arrived next to where she was sitting. "I've got plenty of food if you would like something?" She hesitated.

About to say no thanks, for some unknown reason she relented and allowed him to sit on the ground next to the camping chair. He pulled a container out of his esky and handed it to her. She took a sandwich and handed the container back. Taking a sandwich for himself, he broke off some pieces to feed the ever-grateful Charlie.

She almost groaned out loud as she took a bite of the bread. "This so good. I like the flavour of the chutney. Homemade?"

"Yes, but I can't claim credit. I've been away for a couple of weeks. I picked the food up from my parents along with Charlie, early this morning before I came here."

"Oh, they live nearby?"

"Yeah, I grew up about twenty minutes away from here," he replied, pointing with his sandwich. "Mum always packs enough food to feed a small army. You know, prodigal son returning or something like that." He continued after a short silence, "I noticed the easel in the cabin. Bit of an artist, are you?"

"You could say that," she offered.

"So, you're an artist and your name is Matisse. Rather ironic, isn't it?"

"My mother loved art. Worked in an art gallery for a long time. So, I guess it was natural to come up with the name of an artist for me. It was just coincidental that I happen to paint."

"What does she think of you being here, or doesn't she know?"

"My mother died about ten years ago."

"Sorry to hear that."

She shrugged. "It would have been nice if she'd been there to see my first exhibition, but it wasn't to be."

"What about the rest of your family?"

"There was only ever Mum and me."

The silence was somewhat strained.

"Do you mind if I ask why you picked somewhere like the Cape to come to?"

For a split second, she wavered about throwing it all out there. On the one hand, she wanted to tell someone about what she'd been going through. To talk about Jonno. But she'd only just met this man and she didn't think it would be fair to unburden herself. Although she got the distinct impression he wouldn't mind in the slightest. Something about him made her want to open up, but she quickly shut it down.

"Ah, well, I um, just needed to get away from Sydney for a bit—for some peace and serenity."

"Oh?"

"Yes, well, I needed a change of scenery, somewhere out of the way … and … well … the scenery along the Great Ocean Road is pretty spectacular," she finished lamely.

"Have you been down to the Cape Otway Lightstation yet?"

She shook her head. "Haven't got around to it. Just finding my feet and doing some painting. I haven't been doing much lately—the creativity had pretty well dried up, so if there's even a little spark there I'd like to try and fan it, and keep going if I get on a roll."

"Been too busy to paint?" he asked.

"Not exactly." She wasn't looking at him. "Have had plenty of time, just not the will … I've been in rehab … from an accident." Standing up, Matisse brushed the imaginary crumbs off her lap and walked away following the creek line with Charlie hot on her heels.

~

JAKE HAD SEEN the wall come up. Too much too soon. The accident was obviously still very raw. What sort of accident, he wondered? She obviously wasn't prepared to talk, least of all to a virtual stranger.

He went back to work, but he was distracted, keeping an eye out for her return. Eventually he noticed she was back in the chair with the book on her lap, staring off at the water, playing with a chain around her neck, sliding something back and forth over and over.

Before long, it was late enough to call time on the day. He whistled for Charlie after he packed his ute, but Charlie wasn't forthcoming. He was lying on his back having his tummy rubbed and looked rather sheepish as his owner called him again. Jake walked over to get his dog's attention and to ask her a question.

"Do you mind if I come back tomorrow to replace the rails? That's next on the list." As he'd hoped, she didn't say no.

JAKE MADE an early morning dash into town to stock up his fridge, then called by the bakery to pick up some fresh rolls to go with ham and cheese from the deli. Back at the cabin, he parked alongside the lean-to, his dog jumping out before he'd shut off the engine. Jake followed his four-legged friend.

Charlie received an enthusiastic welcome. His owner, not so much—though she was polite enough. Wearing darker jeans today and another flowing top—this time dark red but still with embroidery around the neckline and hem. Tiny braids on either side of her head came together at the back. Her hair was otherwise loose. There was a bit of a wave in it as it tumbled down her back. He fought the sudden desire to run his fingers through its length to see if her hair was as silky as it looked. She certainly had a natural beauty about her. But there was an underlying current of sadness and vulnerability that seemed to haunt her. He really wanted to find out what was causing her pain. Was it the accident? Was there more to it than her getting hurt? Could someone have died? Maybe she felt responsible? A myriad of questions raced through his thoughts with no answers.

He decided it would be his mission to try and get her to unburden herself. For some reason, he wanted to see her smile. Imagining that got his pulse racing inexplicably.

~

MATISSE DRAGGED an easel down by the water and positioned it carefully, so it was between her and the cabin. She donned one of her painting aprons. It had started out white, but over time had taken on streaks of many other colours.

Choosing paintbrushes to use shouldn't have taken long, but she was trying her best to ignore the very good-looking workman nearby and, to be honest, didn't do very well on that score.

Matisse soon found herself hot and bothered, and not solely due to the unseasonably warm weather. Every other minute she glanced over to where he was working. As he bent to his task of sawing timber she admired, yet again, the way he moved. The way his muscles flexed when he carried the timber to the sawhorse. The action of sawing the wood.

She bit her bottom lip, brushing a colour onto the canvas in front of her. Whatever she was painting—and she had no idea what—didn't bear any resemblance to her usual artistic style. She couldn't help but wonder what it would be like to be held in those strong arms against the hard strength of his chest.

Blowing out a long, slow breath of air, frustrated at her lack of progress on the canvas, Matisse reached for the rag hanging over the side bracket of the worn easel. She wiped the smears off her hands and plunged the brushes into water, leaving their cleaning for later. Checking all the paint tubes were lidded, she pulled off her apron and slung it over the back of the easel, packed up the rest of her gear, and left without a word.

CHARLIE PUT his head up when Matisse started walking. Standing, he shook himself off and followed along behind. Jake let his canine companion go. At least she'd made friends with one of them. Sure, they'd gotten off on the wrong foot when they first met, but he had tried to make up for it since. But she didn't appear to want to have anything to do with him.

Curious, he risked a walk over to her easel, but there wasn't anything much on the canvas he could recognise. She had seemed frustrated when she left—maybe she had "painter's block". Was that even a thing? Or maybe she needed to find herself a muse of some sort—although whether she would find one out here was a moot point. He wondered about her painting style—what techniques she used when she worked. It would be a huge coincidence if she not only shared her name with Henri Matisse but painted like him as well. He was keen to see her work. Maybe not yet—but given time she might come around. Hopefully.

AS THE HAMMERING from the direction of the cabin faded, Matisse slowed her pace and breathed. Jake was too distracting. She would have to come up with some way of banishing him from her line of sight. That would be the easy bit. It was banishing him from her mind that would prove harder to manage.

Charlie nuzzled her hand, disturbing her thoughts, looking for a pat which he duly received. The creek widened and the clear water proved too tempting for the dog, who charged down the bank and splashed in. He turned around and looked at

Matisse as if beckoning her to join him. Laughing at him, she kicked off her shoes and waded in, gingerly at first, the sting of the cold water taking her breath away. The movement of the water as it made its way downstream, tumbling over rocks, soothed her taut nerves. She hadn't realised how tightly wound she was until that moment. Charlie came over with a large stick in his mouth which Matisse obligingly threw for him out on the creek edge. Taking off, he retrieved it and came back to Matisse. The stick went back and forth for a while, until a smell attracted his attention and he disappeared.

Picking up her shoes, she decided to walk back ankle-deep along the edge of the water. Charlie stopped to sniff around trees, and then sprang after her—until he got distracted by something else.

The hammering had stopped altogether, and Matisse quickly found out why. Jake was shirtless, his torso wet, his hair slicked back. He'd obviously used the creek to cool off as well. Matisse felt the colour rise to her face and tried to look away, but was drawn back to the man. All broad-shouldered, smooth-muscled chest with strong arms and a narrow waist ... someone who took good care of himself. She licked her lips nervously and slowed her step.

Charlie took off to his master, who looked first at his dog and then up to see where she was. Matisse had to fight to catch her breath and steady her startled heart as he studied her standing there. Feeling very exposed, Matisse forced herself to walk forward when she really wanted to turn tail and run away as fast as she could. Her eyes followed as Jake turned and strode up the creek bank, bending over as he balanced first on one leg and then the other as he pulled on his boots. Unhurriedly, he reached for his shirt, shaking the material as he slipped it on.

Matisse started to climb up the creek bank and slipped. A hand reached out to grab her, but she refused the offer, knowing his touch would send shock waves through her body as it had before. Clambering out under her own steam, she stood, unsure what to do next. Jake went to his four-wheel drive, pulled the esky out of the back and returned to where she was still standing. He held the container up.

"Lunch?" he queried.

"Um, yeah, sure." He took the esky to the shade and dropped it on the ground near where she'd left her easel. Matisse reluctantly joined him as he pulled out the food and set the lid back down as a makeshift table. He handed her a fresh bread roll with ham and salad which she took, careful to avoid his fingers. *Don't make physical contact,* she told herself. *Don't make eye contact—it's safer that way.*

Jake sat on the ground nearby. Matisse wished he would button up his shirt. Mind you, focusing on the well-toned chest was preferable to those deadly eyes that seemed to see right inside her very being.

She tried to be polite. "So, you said you grew up near here ..."

"Yep. I have an older sister, Andrea, married with two boys and a girl. They live near my parents. My younger sister, Melanie, lives in town with her husband and two kids. And I have a much younger brother as well." Even though he didn't reveal many details, she realised family was very important to him.

After some small talk, he stood to return to the job at hand. Matisse sat glued to her chair as he swung the esky up and sauntered back to his ute, seemingly aware she was watching. He turned back. She dropped her gaze, but felt his eyes on her as he returned to the repair work.

Self-conscious, she fled behind her easel, and Charlie returned to lie down next to her as she absent-mindedly applied paint to the canvas.

CHAPTER THREE

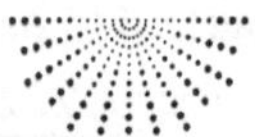

*L*etting himself in the back door of his parents' homestead, Jake followed the noise to the kitchen. His mother was on her way out with a large serving bowl in each hand. Always elegant, Claire Davis wore jeans and a fitted cream blouse with three-quarter-length sleeves. The gold bracelet she'd received for her thirtieth wedding anniversary several years earlier was always on her left wrist. The delicate gold oval locket around her neck had been a gift from her family for her fiftieth birthday.

She caught sight of him as he walked in. "Jacob! Just in time."

"Hi, Mum." He kissed her on the cheek. "Here, let me take those for you." She picked up a couple more dishes and handed them to Andrea as she walked into the room. Older than Jake by three years, Andi was growing more and more like their mother.

"Hey Jakey, welcome back little brother."

"Hi sis." He kissed her on the way past, and then his younger sister Mel as she returned from the dining room. He deposited the bowls on the long timber table and went around to shake hands with his father and brothers-in-law who were already seated.

"Jacob my boy, how was your trip?"

"Yeah, good. Very productive. The new manager has settled in well. We'll be needing another pilot soon, so we will start advertising next month."

Before he had a chance to elaborate further, Claire Davis interrupted. "No business talk at the table, thank you. Sit down. I think we're ready."

Jake high-fived each of his nephews in turn, and returned his nieces' hugs as they took their plates to watch a movie together in the next room. A rare treat. The only one missing from the fortnightly family gathering was Todd, the youngest of Jake's siblings. Dinner tended to be a lively affair, with lots of talk and good-natured teasing back and forth.

When the noise finally abated, Jake said, "I went down to the cabin the other day to do some more work, and found someone living there."

"Backpackers again?" Adam queried.

"No, not this time. A paying tenant."

"I thought you still had a heap to do before it was ready to go?"

"I do."

"So how did that happen?"

"Well, I rang the real estate agent, and it seems their newest staff member is American. You know how they write the date differently to Aussies? She saw the cabin was available from eight-ten. She assumed it was August tenth not October eighth, and went ahead and listed it ... and got a tenant." He ate another mouthful. "This is great, Mum."

"What, even though it's got no electricity or running water?"

Jacob nodded.

"Whoever he is, he must be crazy."

"Except that the tenant is a she, not a he." That got six pairs of eyes looking at him.

Andi's husband was the first to speak up. "Are you going to tell us about her? Did you find out anything?"

"Not much to tell, really. She's an artist, just wanting to escape Sydney for a bit."

"An artist, huh? How old is she?"

"Maybe around your age, Mel."

"Is she good looking?"

"I guess she's okay," he understated. "Charlie seems pretty taken by her though." He feigned disinterest, but could tell his younger sister wasn't convinced.

"Is she short, tall, blonde, brunette?"

He pretended to give it a lot of thought as if he wasn't particularly interested enough to recall. "Um, tallish I guess, long blonde hair."

"And ...?"

"I don't know. Hasn't seen the outdoors much lately I guess." He went back to eating.

"What's her eye colour?"

"Green," he replied, without looking up. Out of the corner of his eye he caught Mel nudging Andi, but ignored them.

"So ... does she have a name?"

"Yeah. It's something to do with an artist, which I thought was a bit ironic seeing as she paints." He paused as if he was trying to remember. "Oh yeah, it's Matisse."

"Does she have a partner?"

"How would I know? I've, like, talked to her a couple of times. She wears plenty of rings, but I didn't notice if one was a wedding band."

"Any family?"

"Jeez, girls, what's with the questions?"

"Seriously? A seemingly eligible female turns up practically on your doorstep. Aren't you just a little bit curious about who she is and her background?"

Of course he was, but he wasn't about to let on to his siblings. "All I know is, she doesn't have any family. It was just her and her mother who died ten years ago, and she was in an accident recently. Quit the interrogation, will you?"

"Okay, okay. Keep your shirt on."

He saw his sisters glance at each other; they definitely knew something was up.

~

Matisse woke with a fright in the very early hours of the morning. It wasn't a nightmare that had woken her, for a change, but an ungodly sound, a deep bellowing noise that escalated to a roar. It seemed to come from different directions. Childhood stories of bunyips, creatures that lurked in billabongs and creeks, came back to her mind as the noise continued. She was not inclined to investigate, and there was nothing she could do to drown the noise out. She wasn't scared—more annoyed than anything. Some sort of animal, she guessed. It kept her from going back to sleep for a long time.

As she lay there listening to the racket, memories of Jonno started running around her head as they did most nights when sleep was elusive. Trying to shove them out of her mind, she redirected her thoughts to her artwork ... what she needed to add to the painting she was working on. At the moment she had three on the go. Sometimes it just worked like that. If she reached a certain point on the canvas and wasn't able to continue, she would start working on something else instead.

"Arghhh, would you just shut up already and give me a break!" she exclaimed in frustration. Moaning she turned over again. "Oh, for crying out loud."

Jake Davis, now there was a thought. As soon as she had seen him, she knew she waited to paint his portrait even though she would never be able to do him justice. Portraiture wasn't her strong suit—she hadn't produced anything yet she would be confident to exhibit with her other work—but maybe somewhere down the track. She enjoyed the challenge though, and Jake Davis would be more than a challenge. Trying to get just the right mix of colours for those gorgeous "melt me" brown eyes of his would be her undoing if she so much as tried to capture him on canvas. She had to admit he was cute. Okay, more than cute. He was very good looking, affable, hardworking —and in other circumstances she might have been a little interested in him. Okay, a lot, if she was truthful. She started to compare Jake with Jonno. "What on earth am I doing? I'm not looking for another relationship. The last one ended tragically and that's it. I can't even think about going down that track again. At all."

Grumbling some more, she grabbed the torch from the floor beside her and headed for the outdoor toilet. Not normally given to leaving the cabin in the middle of the night if she could help it, Matisse slipped her feet into shoes and yanked the door open. The rustling and howling continued to surround her as she stomped down the stairs and across the small patch of grass, wrestling the door open. A few minutes later she crawled back onto the stretcher and slammed the pillow over her head. Maybe she'd need to find some earplugs on her next trip into Apollo Bay.

Finally, the noise outside abated. She guessed the animal had worn itself out. About time! Corralling her thoughts, Matisse eventually drifted off to sleep.

The sleep wasn't anywhere near long enough. It was going to be a struggle this morning to get going. Sighing deeply, she padded to her work area and snatched up a pencil to make some preliminary sketches for a series of paintings she'd planned while staring at the ceiling overnight. She would just have to push through, somehow.

"How's the peace and serenity going for you?" Jake asked when he arrived to find Matisse sitting on the back veranda, instead of at her easel.

"There's not much of that at the moment," she told him, sipping coffee.

He raised an eyebrow.

"Too much carry-on at night. I'm assuming it's probably koalas?"

Jake chuckled. "You're probably right. It is mating season and they do tend to get pretty noisy when they're amorous."

"Great," she groaned, "that's what I thought." She drained her mug. "I think I'm going to need a stronger coffee. Can I offer you one?"

Although he knew it would just be instant and he'd not long finished his own brewed coffee, he readily accepted her offer. She set a second mug down next to where he sat on the newly replaced top step, and retreated to her camping chair. Neither of them spoke for a good few minutes. Relishing the stillness, he breathed in the fresh morning air and the somewhat dubious coffee aroma. He could tell she was savouring her second cup.

Jacob finished the coffee and rose to his feet. "Hey, would you like to take a run over to the Lightstation this afternoon? It only takes about ten minutes to drive from here."

She seemed hesitant, so he sweetened the deal. "If we go just before closing time, I might be able to organise a private tour." Well, he was counting on it, depending on who was working today. Matisse was wary of him, he guessed—with good reason. She hardly knew him yet. He was pretty sure she was edging away from him. Changing his stance, he edged back a little himself. Did she relax? He wasn't sure.

Jacob didn't realise he'd been holding his breath waiting for an answer until she reluctantly agreed to come. Nodding in her direction he turned back to his repair job, looking forward to the excursion and hoping she wouldn't change her mind before then.

~

When Jake packed his gear at the end of the day, he suggested Matisse rug up and bring a camera, if she had one. Charlie was less than impressed to be left behind—tied up, no less. He sulked as his master walked Matisse to the Ranger and opened the door for her.

Noticing Matisse was ill at ease, Jake half expected her to press herself up against the car door, as far away from him as she could get. As it was, she kept her gaze fixed firmly out the side window as they drove. Which in one respect was good, because he could keep stealing glances at her without getting caught. His hand twitched on the steering wheel. It was all he could do not to reach out and see if the skin on her cheek was as soft as it looked. And he wanted to run his fingers down the plait of hair that rested across her shoulder. He forced his hands to hold the steering wheel tighter.

The best course of action was to talk and keep talking, to try to distract himself, but her responses were pretty much all one word. He tried not to be frustrated. The Ranger rumbled over the cattle grid at the white picketed entrance to the Lightstation.

The older woman on duty when they walked into the small white building next to the car park was busy at the till. "I'm sorry, the last tour was at four, and we're closing soon." She looked up. "Jacob! What a surprise to see you." He was greeted like an old friend.

"Good to see you again, Beth," he said. "Busy today?"

"It's okay now, but we've been run off our feet all day. There was a huge line-up before nine. Some sort of holiday in China, so there's been a mass of Chinese tourists through over the last couple of days. It's a long way to travel to Australia for just a few days, but that's how they seem to do things."

Jake noticed Matisse glance around the space crammed with lighthouse souvenirs as he spoke to Beth. Rows of mini light-houses, pencil toppers, fridge magnets, snow domes and model ships. Pretty much anything and everything was either light-house-shaped or had a photo of the Lightstation. As well, there were maps and photos and other higher-end products.

"This is Matisse. She's down from Sydney for a bit. Thought I should bring her out to see the views. Who's up at the light-house today?"

"Simon."

"I was hoping we might be able to look around after you close."

"Sure, I think it'll be okay. I'll just contact him and find out." She picked up the walkie-talkie and soon had an answer.

"Go on through. Take your time—the last group are just on their way down."

Jake led the way to the restored Italian-style Old Telegraph Station. Matisse lingered a few steps behind, taking photos of the white villa surrounded by verandas and topped with a grey-shingled roof. He waited and talked about the building as they walked through the displays on the ground floor. Following the track that led past the head lightkeeper's house, now visitor accommodation, Jacob pointed out other buildings also used for getaways. The cafe in the assistant lighthouse keeper's residence —another white building with a white picket fence—had closed for the day. Its veranda had been enclosed all the way along the front with lots of glass—so the view could still be enjoyed even if the weather wasn't the best. Wooden picnic tables stood beyond the fence line while an Australian flag fluttered from a pole.

The last of the visitors were straggling back as Jacob and Matisse walked out to the lighthouse, along a path bordered on both sides by a white timber railing. As they walked around its base, Matisse craned her head back, positioning the camera to shoot straight up the side of the building. The year 1848, painted red, stood out against the white background.

They climbed seventy-eight stairs to meet their guide.

"Jake, good to see you mate, it's been a while."

"It has. Simon, I'd like you to meet Matisse. She's visiting from Sydney. Going to stay around the area for a while. Beth said you wouldn't mind if we called in."

"No, not at all." He gave Matisse a brief history lesson about the lighthouse as Jake leaned back on the wall and listened to details he was already familiar with. Like the fact it took seventy men ten months to shape the sandstone, and that the lantern was manufactured in London with twenty-one polished reflectors and lamps, and brought ashore in small boats through the crashing water.

Jacob wandered out to the external catwalk that circled the top of the tower, and stood on the ocean side where the wind was blowing strongly. It was brisk out here in the open air. Not that he minded. He pulled his collar up and shoved his hands into his pockets. Matisse followed him outside soon after.

He turned to say something, only to find her pressed up against the lighthouse wall. He stepped over, thinking he might have to peel her off the wall. "Are you okay?"

"Yeah, sure," she lied, "just a bit windy. Makes it harder to adjust the camera settings." She took a deep breath and walked to the railing. Looking out was okay. Looking back to the lighthouse keeper's cottage was fine. Looking straight down on to swirling water crashing on the rocks eighty metres plus below unnerved her a little. She sucked in a deep breath, pulled herself together, and managed to keep going by concentrating on the camera's viewfinder.

Jacob pointed out the newer, much smaller, automated beacon nearby. "Not quite the same, is it?"

"Definitely not as romantic I guess, and nowhere to stand to admire those views."

He led her around to the eastern side and pointed again. "Can you see that building over there?"

"The rectangular blob on the cliff?"

He laughed. "Well, yes. That's my place."

"Seriously?"

"Yes seriously ... and you can see the lighthouse from there."

"The views must be to die for," she told him.

"You should come over sometime."

"I'll think about it. And the cabin?"

He pointed for her. "It's at the other end of the property, about ten minutes that way."

They drove back in the late afternoon sun. Matisse was startled when Jacob suddenly pulled off the road onto a rough, semicircular patch of crushed white gravel.

"What?" She glanced over at him.

"Look there," he pointed. "Koalas. Do you want to take some photos?"

Matisse was out of the car before the words were out of his mouth. She walked to a stand of manna gum trees. There was a koala in a low tree fork, obscured by a branch. Jacob pulled the end of the offending limb down far enough so Matisse could get a clear shot. She gave him a thumbs-up and set off in the direction he indicated, intent on taking more photographs.

OVER THE FOLLOWING days they seemed to fall into a routine. Jacob had usually done a couple of hours' officework before heading down to the cabin, and he did more again in the evenings. The internet made it so much easier to work wherever and whenever he needed.

Matisse was, more often than not, at her easel painting by the time he arrived to start work. Sometimes she was wearing a full-length bib apron of some sort with brushes in the front pocket and maybe a couple of tubes of paint, and always a rag. More often than not, underneath the apron she wore paint-splattered jeans, and an equally splattered grey sweatshirt she peeled off late morning to reveal an oversize t-shirt that made it hard to tell where the abstract print design finished and the paint started. There always seemed to be paint on her hands, around her nails, and often on her face. He was tempted more than once to wipe off her smudges. But that wasn't going to happen.

If she was right in the zone she wouldn't notice he was even there, so intense was her focus. He'd say hello, and if she didn't answer he knew she was absorbed in what she was painting. Then he'd only interrupt her at lunchtime to make sure she ate.

Jacob noticed, however, that she still seemed to want to put space between them if he crossed some sort of invisible line. Initially he thought he was imagining things, but then he decided to test his theory. He deliberately took a step closer and, sure enough, she took a step back. He tried it several times over the next few days, and every time she automatically moved. It became a source of frustration. He wasn't sure what the problem was. She should be used to him by now. To his knowledge, he'd never done anything untoward. Eventually he confronted her.

"Why do you do that?" he asked.

"Do what?" she said.

He took a step towards her and she moved. "That."

"Sorry?"

"You keep moving. Are you scared of me or something?"

She looked up at him, green eyes evidently shocked he had called her out.

"Well?" He waited.

She scraped her hand through her hair then swallowed. "Ah, no."

"Then what?"

"Um, you're messing with my head ... I mean, invading my personal space ... " A hue of pink swept across her face.

Her response indicated she wasn't immune to him. He stepped closer.

She threw a hand up as if to ward him off. "Please don't."

He looked at her standing there, her eyes fixed on the

ground. This time, he was the one who backed away. Would she ever let him get close to her—physically or emotionally? He wouldn't admit to being desperate to find out more about her. Matisse had gotten under his skin in such a short time. He thought about her all the time when he was away from the cabin. Usually he was able to focus on his business with single-mindedness—after all it was how he got to be so successful. Now, his distracted thoughts were hampering his ability to get anything done quickly and decisively.

It bothered him no end that she kept backing away.

Mostly, he felt he was slowly gaining her trust, building a rapport. At least he hoped so.

IT WAS BASICALLY a spur of the moment decision. Jacob was away on a business trip, so Matisse jumped in the van and drove out to see the majestic limestone pillars of the Twelve Apostles—well, the remaining ones that had survived the ocean's scourge at least. She could hardly come all the way to Cape Otway and not make the effort to go that bit further. It was just over an hour from where she was staying.

Jacob had offered to take her, but she always had an excuse not to go. He'd asked if she was scared of him. She wasn't. Just scared of her reaction every time he got too close. It was better that she keep her distance. She found herself attracted to him and was scared she was starting to care. She didn't want to go down that track again. Anytime she caught herself contemplating "that track", she talked herself out of it.

Apparently, the route was not unlike driving the Californian coastal road. She would just take the guidebook's word for it. There were over seven hundred maritime vessels submerged along this stretch of coastline dating from the 1800s and only a third had been found. Staggering. No wonder it was also known as the Shipwreck Coast.

As she followed the Great Ocean Road, Matisse could tell when she was getting close to the Apostles. At least three helicopters were circling overhead, and a small fixed-wing plane cruised along the coastline. She wondered if one of the pilots lived on a property near her cabin as, from time to time, she'd heard a helicopter in the area.

The vehicular traffic became heavier. There were several coaches lined up in one corner of the large carpark, which was at capacity. Matisse had to wait for someone to leave before she could pull in.

Grabbing her camera, she walked to the helicopter charter flight area at the rear of the carpark. The line-up for joy flights was way out the door, with tourists waiting their turn to fly over the Twelve Apostles and along the coast to London Bridge and Loch Ard Gorge. She ducked inside and scanned the list of prices. Ouch, maybe some other time. Standing at the fence, she watched the aircraft come and go. It was crazy—she couldn't believe how busy it seemed to be.

The curve of the galvanised roof on the visitors' centre reminded her of airplane wings as Matisse joined the crowd of people wandering out to the viewing area. The ochre of the rock walls either side of the highway underpass served to highlight the mottled green background of the sign that read: Twelve Apostles, Port Campbell National Park. She followed the boardwalk, but found it difficult to find a vantage spot to take photos —squeezing in between others, jostling for position. The view was well worth it ... but she wasn't coping with the crush of people.

Several tourists handed her their cameras so she could take their picture with the rock formations in the background, although she politely declined the offer to have her own photo taken. Disappointed, she wondered if there was ever a time when it was tourist-free, knowing that she would enjoy the view better in relative solitude.

Deflated, she headed back to the cabin.

CHAPTER FOUR

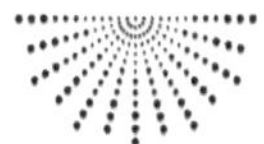

Matisse started to get into a routine for her trips into town. Washing, contacting Max, of course, to let him and Dee know she was still alive, downloading and recharging her camera, catching up with emails and the outside world in general, revelling in the luxury of a comfortable bed and a really long, hot shower ... bliss. She could work the ingrained paint out of her fingers as well, so her body could be paint-free at least for a day, or maybe two.

The green hills on the northern side and the boat harbour to the south bookended the curve of Apollo Bay with its wide sandy beach. She enjoyed wandering down to the water, just to walk or sit. Jonno was never far from her thoughts, although these days there was a bit of competition happening. Jonno no longer held exclusive rights ... there was a certain dark-haired handyman who seemed to be getting a foothold there as well.

But, first thing was to get to the laundry and shove all her clothes in to wash. As the wash cycle began, she returned to her motel room and spread out on the coffee table the brochures she'd picked up at the visitor information centre, to help her explore the area further. She worked her way through them, marking some and discarding others.

One was for another motel on the outskirts of town with an onsite gift shop and art gallery that she was keen to see. She always made a point of visiting galleries to check out the work of local artists wherever she went.

~

MATISSE DRANK in the vista from the Bay View Motel as soon as she pulled the van into their carpark. Glistening blue as far as the eye could see. But with the elevation came the brisk wind chasing her into the white building. Just inside the entrance was the gift shop. Matisse scanned the items on display, but she really wanted to see the artwork. Walking through a doorway into the gallery section, she was quickly absorbed in the artwork and didn't hear the owner approach.

"Hi there, I'm Mel. Welcome to the gallery. Is there anything in particular I can help you with today?"

Matisse turned to the dark-haired woman standing alongside her. She was similar in height and, probably, age. Her long, dark brown hair was pulled back into a high ponytail and she had dark chocolate eyes. Dressed in jeans and a white polo shirt, she seemed friendly enough.

"Thanks, just looking at the moment," Matisse told her. There was no one else in the gallery. The owner went back to sort through some stock on the counter. Matisse couldn't help but glance at her. She seemed vaguely familiar. Matisse reasoned she had probably seen the woman around town and not realised it.

"Are you on holidays?" Mel asked her.

"Not really. I'm here for six months."

"Staying nearby?"

"Out at Cape Otway actually ... I'm an artist."

"You wouldn't be Matisse, by any chance?"

Matisse was surprised. "Yes, how did you know my name?"

"I'm Jacob's younger sister, Melanie. He mentioned there was an artist from Sydney staying in the old cabin down by the creek." As soon as the woman had said she was Jacob's sister, Matisse could see the resemblance.

"Yes, that would be me."

"So how are you coping over there? It's a bit primitive, isn't it?"

"Not any worse than camping, I guess. Although I admit I enjoy staying over in town to have a decent shower and a pub meal, plus a real bed for a night or two. Connect with the outside world and find out what's going on."

"So why are you putting yourself through that?"

Matisse hesitated. "I've been having a tough time. I wanted to get away for a while to hopefully get some peace of mind, and inspiration to paint. I just felt I needed to be on my own for a bit. I've pretty well been surrounded by people 24/7 since ..." She paused. "Well, for a long time."

"So, it's not too isolated for you?"

"It's not as isolated as I thought it was going to be. Your brother has been doing a lot of work on the cabin, so he and Charlie are regular visitors."

"Yeah, he said there'd been some mix-up and you got to rent it before he'd had a chance to finish fixing it up."

"There's quite a long list of things to be done."

"I'd believe it. I don't think anyone has been down there for years. Dad and Jacob used to go there regularly for their boys' weekends, and then Jacob and his mates when they were teenagers."

They chatted amiably for a few minutes. Matisse felt herself warming to Jacob's younger sister.

"Would you like to grab a coffee?" Mel asked her.

"What about the shop?" Matisse queried.

"No problem." Mel walked to the clock sign on the inside of the front door, adjusted the hands to read "back at 11 am" and flipped it over. Mel grabbed her bag and hurried out.

Matisse offered to drive them both back into town.

"Have you been to ABC yet?" Mel said.

"No, what's that?"

"It's short for Apollo Bay Coffee. It's just up here." Melanie pointed as they came closer. Matisse pulled the van into a parking space.

ABC had a relaxed "country meets beach" vibe, like a lot of places in the area. Worn wooden chairs and tables with pale blue cloths dotted the interior. The walls were covered in historic photos of the area.

They both ordered a flat white and a double choc muffin, then chose a table near the window to enjoy the view. Farmland stretched down to the cliff edge. Sheep and other livestock enjoyed commanding ocean views.

"So, tell me about your family," Matisse asked.

"Been married to Adam for almost nine years. He helps run the motel, and is involved in the State Emergency Service. We have two kids, one of each. Ashton is seven and Lily is five. We live on-site. There's a three-bedroom apartment out the back of the reception area. I still do a couple of shifts a week, nursing at the hospital."

"Sounds like it's pretty full-on."

"Yeah, it is, but the family pitch in so we can have a break. Mum and Dad come for a weekend every so often, and Jake is on hand. We also have a very good couple who come and run the place for a week or two—usually over winter when it's a bit quieter—so we can take a holiday. They've been coming for five years now, and it's been a real blessing. They actually have a number of places they visit to do relief work. It works out very well for them."

"Do you have many staff?" Matisse said.

"We don't need very many. There are a couple of people who help with the cleaning and the yard work, and some part-timers to work in the gallery. You know, we could display some of your work if you're interested."

"Thanks, I'll keep it in mind."

"So, where do you stay when you're in town?"

"Oh, here and there. I haven't got a preference—whatever is available."

"You should come and stay with us. We can make it a regular booking in one of the rooms, if you like. Why don't you check them out, and you can pick one?"

"Sounds good to me."

After a tour of the rooms, Matisse chose one of the quieter ones on the far end of the complex, with a queen-size bed that would be a luxury after her narrow camp stretcher, and a decent-sized bathroom. A small table and chairs sat just outside the door to take advantage of the water view.

Mel wrote up her booking information. "That's all set for next week. Why don't you come for dinner tonight, and meet Adam and the kids?"

Matisse hesitated to accept, but she could do with a bit of company.

A TALL, athletic, very good-looking man with cropped blond hair opened the door when Matisse turned up at six-thirty. His friendly blue eyes were enhanced by the blue of his t-shirt. He wore trackpants with it, and canvas lace-ups that had definitely seen much better days.

"Hi, you must be Matisse. I'm Adam." He shook her hand and opened the door wider for Matisse to follow him inside.

Melanie greeted her warmly, gesturing to a stool at the bench, across from where she was working. "Dinner's almost ready." Adam disappeared to allow them to chat, and Matisse took in her surroundings. It wasn't as small as she had expected, and looked to have been recently renovated. The kitchen itself was quite modern with stainless steel appliances. Mel had changed into a black singlet top under an open teal checked shirt. Her hair was held back by a teal patterned scarf. Matisse chatted easily with Jacob's younger sister and before long was helping to serve the meal as Mel called for the others.

Lily had inherited her father's blond good looks, while Ashton was dark like his mother. Matisse could see the resemblance to his Uncle Jake.

"Matisse is an artist. She does a lot of paintings," Melanie told the pair. "She lives out near Nanna and Grandad and Uncle Jake."

Mel served a chicken pasta bake with salad and some soft dinner rolls warm from the oven. Dessert was apple crumble topped with custard and vanilla ice cream.

Before too long, Matisse felt right at home. She enjoyed Adam and Mel's company and quickly made friends with Ashton and Lily. So much so that at bedtime she was elected to read a story. Later, once it quietened down, the three adults enjoyed a relaxing coffee out in the lounge. Mel curled up next to Adam. It was hard not to be just the tiniest bit jealous of their obviously loving relationship. Matisse mainly talked about her artwork, and deflected as much attention as she could from her personal life.

But the question came anyway. "Jacob mentioned you were in an accident?"

"Ah … yes …" She hesitated. "Look you may as well know … it was in Bali. My fiancé, Jonathan, was driving a scooter— with no helmet, as tourists tend to do in Bali. He died. I was pretty badly injured."

"Oh Matisse, I'm so sorry."

"Thanks. I'm still trying to come to terms with it—although the accident was almost two years ago. Staying out at the cabin is part of that process. Living a pared-back lifestyle is helping me focus on my painting. Fewer distractions. No electricity—therefore no phone, no television."

"Do you think it's helping?"

"I'm not sure yet, to be honest. Mostly it's just me and my

easel—but sometimes my thoughts could do with some distracting."

"I don't doubt it's a double-edged sword. The things that distract you from painting no doubt are the same things that distract you from dark thoughts."

Matisse steered the conversation away from her personal life and stayed with the couple way later than she intended, but looked forward to spending more time with her new-found friends.

~

BACK AT THE CABIN, unpacking was a slow job, sorting and storing everything. Finally, it was done. She wandered over to her creative corner, picked up a paintbrush and was quickly absorbed in the canvas, not looking up again until it was too dark to see what she was doing.

Sighing, she went to find the camping light, weighing up whether to continue painting for a bit longer. If she gave into the temptation to keep going, she knew she would forget to sleep. It was bad enough that she forgot to eat at times, but she'd promised Max she wouldn't forsake sleep. Reluctantly she lidded the paint and cleaned the brushes before turning in for the night.

When Matisse walked outside in the morning, she noticed it. Under the tree where she habitually sat was a timber bench with a seat cushion running its length. Walking over to take a closer look, she noticed a white envelope attached to the back-rest. No guesses needed about where it had come from. The note inside was brief.

I know this is your favourite spot, so I thought you might appreciate this. Enjoy, J.

Admiring the timber work as she ran a hand over its smoothness, she tested it out for a few minutes before fetching a book, and settling in. Putting a pillow against the armrest, she lifted her feet onto the bench and leaned back, her book resting on bent knees. Breathing deeply, she enjoyed the early morning breeze. A little distracted, expecting her daily visitors, she reread the same few pages several times, and still didn't follow the storyline.

Soon enough, she heard Jacob's four-wheel drive pull up. And then Charlie came and found her.

JACOB WAS PLEASED to see she was already ensconced on the seat. Mind you, she didn't move her legs so he could join her. He regarded her for a minute, as she reached over to welcome his dog. Her hair was wound up into a bun, and he admired the curve of her exposed neck as she leaned down to pat Charlie. He wished he could just lean down and ... he pulled his thoughts back into line.

"Hey, I see you're not painting this morning yet."

"No, I wanted to try this out," she indicated the seat.

"And?"

"And it's perfect. Thanks for thinking of it. What a lovely piece of furniture. Where did you get it?"

"It's actually timber from here. Left over from the logging days. Instead of letting it rot where it fell, I decided to have some furniture made. It's one of a matching pair. The other is up at my place where you can sit and admire the ocean view." He paused. "I heard you met my sister and her family."

"What? Oh, yes, as a matter of fact I did."

"And ...?"

"And they seem quite nice."

He knew from a phone call that Matisse had already received the tick of approval from his sister. He was pleased that Matisse seemed to get on well with Mel, Adam and the kids. From past experience, he knew it wouldn't be worth his while to pursue a relationship with someone who didn't pass muster with his family—particularly Mel, who he was closest to. Likewise, if Matisse didn't like Mel, he couldn't see himself hanging around. *Whoa! Pursue a relationship with Matisse?* He guessed he *was* interested enough to see where things could lead.

They chatted a while about Mel's family before Jacob changed the subject. "I'm looking to replace the cabin roof next."

"What? No way! It will take away from the character of the place."

He was taken aback by her sudden vehemence. "You won't appreciate the character of the place when it starts raining and you get wet ... inside." She wasn't having any of it, so he tactfully dropped the matter. There were plenty of other jobs he could go on with.

MATISSE DIDN'T BELIEVE him about the leaking roof until she got splattered in the middle of the night. Waking up with a start as cold drops hit her face, she moved her camp stretcher several times as one place after another started to drip. Grumbling as the rain got heavier and the number of drips increased, she stumbled around, still half asleep, gathering her artwork together to move it away from the water. Pulling a tarp out, she covered her canvases just to be on the safe side, and pulled a smaller one over herself. It was a long, uncomfortable night.

In the morning, after the rain had stopped, she waited damp and miserable on the top step.

By the time Jacob arrived she was contrite.

"You were right," she told him as soon as he got out of the Ranger. "When do you want to replace the roof?"

HE GRINNED as he helped her empty the containers she had

scattered around the cabin to catch all the leaks, and they pulled her gear out to dry in the sun. The makeshift clothesline was full, as was the veranda railing, so he spread some of it over the front of his four-wheel drive.

The roof repairs were going to be a bigger job than Jacob could manage on his own, so he enlisted the help of his father, and his brother-in-law Sam. Once the supplies arrived, he organised for Matisse to spend a couple of days in Apollo Bay so they could get a clear run at the roof. There'd be less distraction for him that way.

Sam and Jake's father arrived at first light, unloaded their tools and got stuck into the job at hand. Matisse had moved her art gear to one corner of the cabin, and he had re-tarped it all. Her clothes and other belongings were also under cover.

Once the roof was removed, the remaining structure was covered for the night. The three of them had brought sleeping bags to camp out overnight in readiness for an early start.

It was a huge effort, and Jacob was glad of the extra help—especially as his thoughts were scattering all over the place. Everywhere he looked he could visualise Matisse. Painting mostly. Playing with his dog. Sitting by the water's edge. Reading. And occasionally, very occasionally, even helping him out by holding something that he honestly didn't need help with. The ploy had encouraged her to come a little closer and actually interact with him. He'd also done other things to make it more pleasant for her, such as re-rigging the solar camping shower without being asked, and even making a privacy screen for her. Not that she ever used it while he was around, but he was sure it gave her more peace of mind.

He wondered what she and Mel were up to, seeing as they had become firm friends in the last few weeks. Probably rehanging the artwork in the gallery for a better visual flow. Or changing the stock display in the gift shop. They had done that a couple of times already when new products had arrived. Mel was pleased to have Matisse cast her artistic eye over the layout. She was even making plans for Matisse to supply some artwork to go in the hotel rooms.

Maybe he could commission her to do some work for a few of his business enterprises—for the reception areas. He'd have to see her work of course. No, actually he wouldn't care—he'd be happy to support her, sight unseen. Would she appreciate the gesture? He hoped so.

"Hey, Jake!"

"Huh?"

"Get with the program, man." His brother-in-law wasn't impressed. Was he that distracted? That was the third time Sam had admonished him in an hour. Man, he needed to pull it together. Fast.

By the time Matisse arrived back late the next afternoon they were just finishing up.

With her hands full, she walked around the back of the cabin, almost tripping over Charlie who was trying to get her attention for a pat. Jacob rescued a cooler bag and cake tin from her hands before they ended up on the ground. She bent to pat Charlie. "Hey boy, how's it going?"

"We're pretty much done," Jacob told her.

She surveyed the roof. "Um. It still looks the same."

"No, it's actually a new roof."

"You're kidding?"

He shook his head. "I managed to source some old sheets of roofing iron that were still in pretty good nick. I had them treated so they still maintain the rustic look but won't deteriorate and let the rain in."

"I'm seriously impressed."

Jacob took her to meet the other men. "Matisse this is my father, James."

"Hi Mr Davis, thanks for coming to help out."

"My pleasure, Matisse, lovely to meet you. Jacob has mentioned you once or twice." He smiled at her with a twinkle in his eyes.

James Davis was a thinner, older version of his son. He had the same dark brown eyes, albeit framed with glasses, and remnants of the same dark hair, which was still thick but mostly grey.

Jacob gestured to the other man. "This is Sam, who is married to my older sister Andrea."

Matisse shook hands with the brown-haired, stockily-built Sam, who she guessed was around the forty-year mark.

"You have all done an awesome job; the roof looks great. It blends in with the original building and doesn't stick out like a sore thumb." She walked down to the creek to have a look from a different angle.

Jacob walked with her to survey the finished job. "Well?"

"I wasn't looking forward to seeing a shiny, gleaming roof on the old structure, but this ... is perfect. I'm so grateful that you've kept the integrity of the place." She looked at it for a long time. "Oh. I almost forgot—Mel sent some food out for dinner. I can get it ready if you want to finish up."

Jake and Sam carried the bench seat over from the creek to sit on, James Davis made himself comfortable in the camping chair, and Matisse perched on the steps. They set up a couple of camping lights as the sun went down. The insulated bag had kept the meal warm, and luckily Matisse had a picnic set of place settings to use. The men were mostly quiet as they ate the beef casserole, which suited her fine. Afterward, Matisse cut large slabs of chocolate cake for the other three to devour.

"Whoa, Mel sent chocolate cake!" Sam exclaimed.

"Mel is renowned in our family for her chocolate cake," Jacob explained. "Mum does an awesome sponge cake and Andrea's specialty is lemon meringue pie."

"What about my chocolate brownies?" Sam wanted to know.

"Oh yeah, and Sam the Man here does a pretty mean chocolate brownie. He can only do one dessert, by the way."

"Well that's one more than you, my friend," Sam retorted.

"I'll just stick to the mains, mate."

"You and me both," Jake's father added.

"Oh, this cake is delish," Matisse exclaimed as she savoured the last of her portion.

Jake came over to where she was sitting to claim a second helping.

"Leave some for the rest of us," she told him.

He waved the wedge he'd just cut in front of her mouth, teasing her.

She grabbed his arm to keep it still while she nabbed a mouthful, laughing. Then she made the mistake of looking up. Even in the camping lights, his eyes were pulling her in.

"You have some icing on the top of your mouth," Jake said quietly.

Was she imagining things, or did he lean in slightly … as if he might …

Matisse blinked.

Jake cleared his throat.

Matisse pushed off the step as she wiped her mouth.

If the other two hadn't been there …

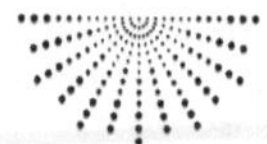

CHAPTER FIVE

Matisse pulled into the Bay View Motel and reached over to grab the casserole dish Mel had asked her to return. She knocked and kept walking in as she usually did, calling out as she went. "Hey, Mel. It's me."

She stopped abruptly.

Mel wasn't there.

Jake was.

He was standing at the kitchen bench, looking like the next Chesty Bond model. A little scruffy this morning, unshaven and barefoot in navy boxer shorts with a white singlet. Lily was on a chair beside him, wielding a spatula. They wore matching red aprons—Jake's a little too small and Lily's way too big. The ties went around her middle a couple of times. The ties around Jake barely made it into a small bow.

Uncle Jake looked right at home supervising his niece. Matisse realised she may have been staring at them—okay, staring at Jake. She swallowed.

"Um, Mel asked me to drop this around this morning," she told him, waving the dish in her hand.

"She's not here. Went to Melbourne the day before yesterday, with Adam."

"That's funny, she didn't mention anything when I saw her. She specifically said to bring it back today. I didn't see the Ranger out front." *If I had, I could've been better prepared.*

"I'm parked out back."

~

JACOB TURNED the pan off and pulled Lily off the chair. "We'll finish cooking in a minute," he told his niece.

Matisse looked decidedly uncomfortable. Jake wasn't sure whether to be pleased or annoyed at his sister's meddling. It could go either way, depending on how Matisse reacted.

"It's their wedding anniversary and Melbourne was planned a while back. Sorry, Matisse, I think we've been set up."

Her face flushed as his words sank in. "Oh, I see. Well then. I'll just leave it here and you can let her know I called round."

"Now that you're here, why don't you stay for breakfast?" He turned to Ashton and Lily. "What do you think, guys, should Matisse stay?" He figured she wouldn't refuse them, and he was right. The kids didn't have to beg too hard.

Ashton and Lily cheered.

"What's on the menu this morning?" she asked.

"Hash browns and bacon and tomato," Lily told her as Uncle Jake lifted her onto the chair and turned the pan back on. Matisse looked at Ashton.

"Do you need a hand there, Ash?"

"Can you get the plates, please?"

Jake opened the crockery cupboard and pointed for Matisse then went back to supervising Lily. He handed the five-year-old a pair of tongs, and held a serving plate for the bacon, then the tomato and hash browns. Lily climbed down from her spot and took the plate from Jake. Jacob threw his apron on the bench and untied Lily's so she could sit comfortably. Ashton came to the table with a red plastic squeeze bottle of tomato sauce and poured it liberally over his hash browns.

Jacob tipped some out for Lily. "More please, Uncle Jake."

He obliged. "Just don't tell your mum how much I'm letting you have, okay?"

Matisse and Jacob both reached for the tongs at the same time.

"You go," he told her, pushing the plate toward her.

MATISSE PUT some hash brown in her mouth while Lily waited and watched. Matisse knew she was expecting a compliment about her cooking.

"Lily, these hash browns are really yummy. Good job, chef." The little girl beamed at her.

Ashton and Lily were very chatty, as was Jacob. Matisse less so. She felt awkward intruding on their time together.

After they had eaten, Ashton took the plates to the sink.

"Can we still go fishing, Uncle Jake?" he pleaded.

"Sure thing, as soon as the dishes are done, and we clean up the kitchen."

Lily tugged at Matisse's elbow, "Will you come too, Matisse?"

Matisse hesitated, but in the end she couldn't say no to those blue eyes.

"Can you leave the motel?" she asked Jake as they worked together to clean up from breakfast.

"No problem. By the time these guys are changed and sunscreened up, the day manager should be here."

JAKE WAS PLEASED Lily had invited Matisse—it saved him having to do it. It would give them a chance to spend time together in a different setting.

Hopefully, Matisse would relax. She was obviously a little

uncomfortable over breakfast. It was understandable—after all, she had been ambushed by Mel and then by Ashton and Lily. There was no way he was going to complain. He was looking forward to the rest of the morning and would just have to see what transpired.

He returned to the living room in denim shorts and a light grey polo shirt, swinging a large pump bottle of sunscreen by the handle. Jacob started applying sunscreen to Ashton. Matisse followed suit and smothered Lily, who rolled her eyes. The adults also applied their own sunscreen.

Jacob slapped a black cap on his head, handed the kids their hats, then tossed a navy cap at Matisse. She put it on her head, then pulled it off and adjusted it before pulling her ponytail through the gap at the back and settling it on her head.

"Okay, you lot, let's go."

They crossed the road and joined the path that headed down the stairs to the beach. Lily carried a bucket and spade as she skipped alongside Matisse, who had been given responsibility for a bag with extra towels, sunscreen and water bottles. Jacob and Ashton, each with a towel around their neck, walked ahead, discussing their fishing plans.

MATISSE COULDN'T HELP herself as her eyes roamed up and down Jacob's figure. Okay, he was one hot-looking guy. He filled out that polo shirt—just right.

There weren't many people around, so they had no problem staking out a spot. The boys threw their towels in a pile next to the bag Matisse had dropped. Ashton called for his uncle, as Lily attempted to push Matisse down the beach to the water.

"Settle down you kids—there's no hurry," Uncle Jake told them.

Lily hopped from one foot to another as her uncle crouched down and baited a hook for her. He cast the line out and stood behind her, passing the black kid-sized rod over. The little girl kept up a steady stream of chatter while Jacob helped her manipulate the rod and reel. Ashton concentrated on the line stretched from his own red fishing rod.

MATISSE STOOD TO ONE SIDE, content to let her feet sink in the wet sand and have the cool water swirl around her ankles, enjoying the gentle breeze and the warmth of the sun on her body.

It wasn't long before Lily became bored with fishing, and Jacob took over her rod. Lily pulled at Matisse's hand, to go with her to search the rock pools. They collected shells and pebbles, twigs, bits of seaweed and even a feather.

Matisse enjoyed the little girl's company even though she talked nonstop. At least she was learning a bit more about Uncle Jake. Lily, along with her brother, obviously idolised him.

JACOB WATCHED from a distance as Matisse bent down next to his niece. The two girls seemed to be getting along famously. Lily, cute in her pink t-shirt and floral hat, held up what appeared to be a shell and dropped it into her bucket.

Matisse was also cute in her fringed shorts. He'd noticed the scar that ran partway down her left leg. It started somewhere under the edge of her shorts and stopped mid-calf—a legacy from the accident, he assumed. Still, he couldn't help but admire her.

Okay, she was more than cute. It had been a long time since a female had captured his interest, and Matisse certainly drew him in.

He could easily picture the two of them spending long summer afternoons on the beach with their own children.

Jacob was surprised at the direction his mind had taken. He shook himself out of his reverie as Matisse walked over with Lily trailing behind.

"I think we might go for a wander to the s-h-o-p-s," she spelt out, "and get some i-c-e c-r-e-a-m."

"Sure." He nodded and reached for his wallet, but she waved him away.

"No, it's okay, I've got it."

Her fingers flicked his and it was all he could do not to rub at the spot on his hand, tingling from that brief touch. He wanted to gaze into the greenness of her eyes, if only for a moment, but she wouldn't look at him.

"C'mon Miss Lily, let's go." She turned quickly and held out a hand, waiting for Lily to catch up.

Jake couldn't help but watch as they wandered along the beach and up the stairs. He sighed to himself. The kids had warmed to Matisse quickly. So had he.

Ashton called him to come and help. Shaking his head to try and clear his thoughts of Matisse, he jammed his rod into the sand and hurried to his nephew.

SPACE, I need some space. He's messing with me again.

Matisse was acutely aware of Jacob's gaze on her when she walked away with Lily. Resisting the urge to turn around, she tugged at the little girl's hand in an attempt to hurry her along.

Matisse and Lily made their way across to the nearby shops. There was a newsagent, convenience store, and takeaway, as well as an ice cream shop servicing the nearby caravan park. The girls mooched around the newsagent. For a small beachside community, it was a large shop, with rows of greeting cards and magazines. A large gift and souvenir section opposite the counter no doubt catered to the tourists who would flock there in the coming summer months. Matisse found a couple of magazines and picked up a novel at the back of the store in the small section of books. She let Lily choose an activity book that came with a little box of six colouring pencils glued to the front.

The bespectacled shop assistant recognised Lily as Matisse placed her purchases on the counter. "Why hello there, Miss Lily." He had thinning salt and pepper hair and wore a mono-grammed dark green polo shirt.

"Hello, Mr O'Brien."

"I see you have a friend with you today."

"That's Matisse, she lives with Uncle Jake."

"Lily!" Matisse was incredulous. "That's not true, I don't live with your Uncle Jake. I live near him."

Mr O'Brien raised an eyebrow at her. Embarrassed, Matisse took the brown paper bag of reading material and shoved the credit card back in her purse, almost yanking the little girl out of the newsagent. Once they were out of earshot, Matisse admon-ished the five-year-old.

"Lily, please don't tell people I live with your Uncle Jake. He comes and visits, but he doesn't live with me. Just like he visits you sometimes, but he doesn't actually live with you."

Confused, Lily looked at Matisse. "But he sleeps over some-times. Does he sleep over at your place, too?"

"No, Lily, he doesn't."

Lily just shrugged. "Okay."

They stopped next door to buy the ice creams. The long narrow shop had three or four white vinyl-covered tables crowded between the large front window and the counter. Old-fashioned booths, several of which were occupied by young families, ran along the wall opposite the counter. High on the wall behind the counter, a chalked menu displayed ice cream flavours which could go into cones, cups, sundaes or as part of the inevitable soft drink/ice cream combination known as a spider. The double row of flavours in silver cans stretched across two display cases. According to the salesgirl's boast, all of the ice creams and sorbets were made on the premises with local ingredients, and the myriad of choices changed according to the seasonal availability of ingredients.

Lily climbed up on the raised viewing platform, built at the front for children to see into the freezer. Matisse let Lily choose the flavours for everyone. Matisse juggled the bag from the newsagent and two cones, while Lily insisted on carrying two herself. They hightailed it back to the beach, with Lily stopping every so often to lick the dripping ice cream. Matisse ended up doing the same.

When they made it back to the boys, Lily handed a cone to her brother, who promptly complained that it had been licked.

"It's okay mate, Matisse has done the same to mine. I don't think they had a choice, the ice cream melted way too fast."

When Jake took the offered cone from Matisse, his fingers brushed hers and stayed there until she let go. They locked eyes briefly. Her stomach fluttered and she hitched a breath, turning her focus to the ice cream.

"Sorry, Lily decided you should have bubblegum flavour."

HE SHRUGGED and started to eat his cone, all the while watching her eat. He couldn't figure out how she managed to look sexy licking ice cream. But she did. It set his pulse racing, and Jacob had to force himself to look away.

"Bubblegum, Lily, my favourite. How did you know?"

Lily laughed. "Because I'm clever."

A few minutes later, Jake retrieved a bottle from the carry bag, pulled a handkerchief from the pocket of his shorts and soaked it with water. Beckoning his niece over, he wiped the sticky mess off her face and hands. Ashton also used the wet handkerchief to clean up. Matisse crouched to dip her hands into the salt water, shaking them off and drying her hands on the back of her shorts.

It looked like fishing was done for the day, so the four of

them meandered up the beach. Ashton and Lily chased each other and seagulls along the water's edge. Jacob mostly told tales about his two charges. As they walked, he accidentally-on-purpose brushed up against her more than once, keeping his hands firmly in his pockets to try and counter the strong desire he had to grab her hand and pull her in against his side. Sometimes the breeze blew strongly enough to carry her scent to him, and he hoped it wasn't obvious that he was inhaling deeply, trying to capture another whiff of coconut and frangipani.

LUNCH SOON BECKONED. Ashton and Lily complained they were totally starving, so Matisse volunteered to return to the shops for fish and chips. After scanning the chalkboard menu, she made a choice, then sat and read an old magazine at one of the outside tables while waiting for her number to be called. A line of people started to form inside—she had made it just ahead of the lunchtime rush. Thankfully, it wasn't long before her order was called.

Pausing at the top of the stairs with her fish parcel, Matisse scanned the beach. Jacob and Lily stood talking to an older couple. Lily showed them something then ran down to the water's edge where her brother was digging with a stick in the sand. The fish and chips were starting to burn her hands through the white paper wrapping as she walked over to Jacob. He introduced the couple.

"This is Bob and Lois, from Queensland, Ipswich actually, doing the grey nomad thing and travelling clockwise around Australia." Bob had a khaki bucket hat in his hand and was fiddling with one of the many souvenir travel pins decorating the crown. Putting it back on his head, he reached out to shake her hand. He wasn't very tall, and his navy checked shirt seemed a couple of sizes too big—as if he was expecting to grow some more. Maybe he was planning to eat a lot on this trip. Lois wore a floral-banded bucket hat and, to be honest, looked a little like a liquorice allsort in her multi-hued polo shirt.

Lois raised the drawstring bag that seemed to contain their shoes in the direction of Ashton and Lily. "I was just telling your husband what delightful children you have."

"Oh, but they're …" She felt a slight pressure on the small of her back from Jacob's hand. "Yes … they are, thank you." She shot him a "what's going on" look but he wasn't paying attention.

"Your little boy looks just like his dad."

"Actually," Matisse told the elderly woman, "most people seem to think he looks more like his uncle." Two could play at this game she thought, glancing at Jake.

Lois peered at Matisse closely. "Such a shame neither of them has your lovely eyes."

"Well, maybe next time," Jacob said, unexpectedly putting his free hand on Matisse's stomach and patting it.

"Jacob!" Matisse wasn't sure what shocked her most: what he said or what he did. Her hand moved automatically to bat his away, but as soon as she made contact with him it was like she had superglued her hand to his and couldn't move it.

IF YOU HAD ASKED HIM, Jake would have had no logical explanation why he responded to Lois the way he did. He wasn't sure who was more surprised—Matisse or himself. Whatever had prompted him to react that way? Wishful thinking?

"Oh, congratulations. What are you hoping for this time? A boy or a girl? Bob and I have two of each, all grown up of course and married—with eleven grandchildren between them."

"One of each actually," Jacob told the elderly woman, with a straight face.

There was a sharp intake of air from Matisse.

He decided he was enjoying himself, hugely.

Lois looked blank, but only for a second. "Twins! Oh how lovely. You're hardly showing at all dear—I can hardly tell you are pregnant."

"We only just found out—nobody knows yet. Sorry sweetheart," he rested a cheek on the top of her head briefly, "I just had to tell someone."

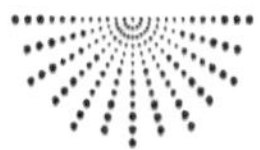

Seriously! Oh my goodness, what was he thinking? Why?
Fragmented thoughts fought for attention in her brain. Matisse was relieved Ashton and Lily were out of earshot.

"Well, it was nice to meet you both." Matisse tried to end the conversation and move out of Jacob's grasp, but his hand slid from her back up to her shoulder.

The older couple finally went on their way. Matisse was stunned. *What just happened?*

Jacob took the parcel out of her hands and called Ashton over. "Here buddy, catch!" He tossed the fish and chips to him. "Now you can truthfully say you caught the fish for lunch."

Ashton grinned at him and headed for a shady picnic table up on the grassed area with Lily close behind him.

"What was that in aid of?" she demanded under her breath.

"They assumed, and I just didn't bother to correct them. I figured it was easier than trying to explain they were my niece and nephew and you were some random artist—not my wife or even my girlfriend."

"Don't you think the twin thing was going a bit far?"

He shrugged. "What will it matter? We won't see them again." He wasn't about to apologise. Yes, he had pushed the boundaries, but it was worth it to get a little closer to her, if just momentarily. Hopefully she would get over it.

They joined the other two at the timber table. Ashton had already opened the wrapper. He and Lily were sitting together helping themselves.

"Hey, you're supposed to wait for us," Jacob told them, threading his long frame through the gap between the table and the bench. He noticed Matisse sat reluctantly on the end without tucking her legs underneath, as if she was getting ready to do a runner. Apportioning out the fish, he handed a wedge of lemon to Lily who squeezed some juice on her fish.

"Ow! Uncle Jake, I got some in my eye. It's stinging! Ow, ow!"

"Hang on, kiddo."

She ran around to where he was sitting, rubbing her eye. Jacob used the end of his polo shirt to wipe her eye. She screwed her face up, and jigged up and down.

"Hold still a minute. Lily!" He raised his voice, but she wasn't listening. Jacob pulled himself out of the seat and picked Lily up under one arm. He took her to a nearby tap and flushed her eye out.

Matisse watched the scene play out. Jacob got down on Lily's level and put his hands on her shoulders, talking to her quietly. Lily nodded and flung her arms around his neck. He hugged her and then stood up and walked back, holding her hand.

"Are you okay now?" Matisse asked.

"Yes," Lily said shyly.

Jacob lifted her up on to the seat between them and put some food in her place on a section of the paper.

It was quiet for a few minutes as they ate. Matisse suddenly had a revelation that surprised her. This is what life might be like if she did in fact "live with Uncle Jake" as Lily had put it earlier. Family time at the beach, enjoying each other's company. The simple pleasures of fish and chips wrapped in white paper …

She looked up as Jacob said her name.

"Matisse, where are you? Come back."

She coloured, hotly embarrassed. Jacob gave her a quizzical look. Needing a distraction, she reached for a paper serviette to wipe her hands.

MATISSE HADN'T PLANNED on staying longer after they returned to the motel, it just happened. Not that she minded. Jacob had excused himself to shower and change, and then been called to the front desk before he could get Ashton and Lily sorted. By default, it fell to Matisse to get them showered and settled.

She played card games with the kids while Jacob was in and out as people arrived to be checked in. The motel would be fully occupied tonight.

JACOB STOPPED in the doorway for a minute. Ashton, hair still damp, in his favourite Aussie cricket t-shirt, sat cross-legged on a lounge chair reading. Lily, in a lilac sundress, her hair in two little plaits, was at the table colouring in with Matisse, their heads bent close together, talking quietly.

It was a heart-warming domestic scene that he suddenly realised he desperately wanted for himself.

Matisse looked up and caught him out. He started moving and asked Ashton about the book, taking it out of his hands to flick through the pages just to give himself something to focus on. Wandering on to the kitchen, Jacob grabbed a tall glass and filled it with iced water.

~

MATISSE NOTICED Jake had stretched himself out on the couch, with his feet propped up on the armrest. He appeared to be asleep.

She untaped the feather from the collage she'd helped Lily make from the bits and pieces they'd scavenged from the beach, and gave it to Lily with instructions. The little girl used it to good effect, waving it under her uncle's nose and brushing it against his cheek. Lily stifled a giggle as her uncle, eyes still closed, swatted at the feather. She grinned at Matisse.

Jake suddenly roared to life, scaring both Lily and Matisse in the process. Grabbing Lily, he hoisted her above him into the air as she screamed and laughed. Managing to get to his feet, he plonked his niece down on the couch and stood in front of her, hands on hips. He chastised Lily in mock anger.

"Now Miss Lily, tell me the truth, was this your idea?" Lily looked from her uncle to Matisse, giggling.

The five-year-old shook her head and pointed. "It was Matisse."

Jake bent down and whispered in the little girl's ear. She grinned at him nodding. He stood up and took a step within arm's reach of Matisse.

"You know what that means, Lily?"

"Ticklefest!" they both shouted in unison.

Before Matisse could react, Jacob had a hold of her so Lily could tickle her. The next thing, Matisse was on her back on the couch, Lily on top of her with Ashton joining in. Jacob knelt beside the couch, and the three of them let her have it. Fighting for a breath, she laughed and begged for mercy, but got none.

"What in the world is going on here?"

Lily stopped mid-tickle. "Daddy, you're home! Hooray,

Mummy's back." Lily climbed down and raced over to hug her parents.

Jacob released Matisse, pulled her upright, and clambered up looking a bit sheepish. Matisse tried to straighten her clothes and smooth her hair. Both Adam and Melanie seemed to be trying to keep a straight face.

"Lily, you were supposed to keep an eye on Uncle Jake. It looks like he's been a bit naughty." Adam winked at his daughter.

"Matisse started it," Jacob said in his defence. "She encouraged your daughter to attack me while I was asleep."

"Yeah, with a feather," Matisse retorted.

Adam hammed it up, putting his hands up to silence them all.

"I don't care who started it. You are all in trouble."

Lily was enjoying the drama. Melanie threw her brother a grin.

Matisse recovered first. She coughed, ignoring Adam and Jacob, and went over to Mel.

"So how was Melbourne? What did you get up to?"

Mel took her arm and steered her away. "Dinner and a show, among other things." She smiled.

After catching up with Mel for a few minutes, Matisse made to leave.

"Are you sure you don't want to stay for dinner?"

"Thanks, but I'd better go. I want to be back before it gets dark. Say goodbye to the others for me."

"I hope you had a good day with Jacob and the kids."

"Mmm. It was quite nice—not sure I approve of your methods though."

Melanie just smiled at her friend. "You can thank me later."

Matisse just shook her head.

~

JACOB ARRIVED at the van just as Matisse opened the driver's door. "Hey Matisse, thanks for hanging out with us today."

"That's okay."

"You were good company."

"Ashton and Lily are terrific kids; you are lucky to have them for a nephew and niece. Lily is such a delight. I hope I get one like her one day."

"Same," he told her. There was a bit of an awkward silence.

"Anyway, I'd better be going."

"Okay, thanks again." He patted her arm and went back inside. He fought the urge to turn around and watch her go—he didn't want her to drive away, but he wasn't going to stop her leaving. He'd given her enough to think about for one day. The shocked look she'd thrown him when he put his hand on her stomach pretending they were having twins was priceless. Come to think of it—he wished it were true.

He'd not given much thought to having his own family—he'd been too busy building his business. Plus, he'd never met anyone who made him think about starting a family—until now. If only he could convince her to take a chance on him—but that would mean moving on from Jonno and, well, that was the point. Would she ever be ready to move on from Jonno?

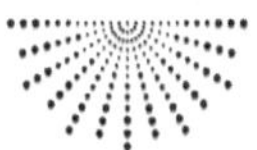

ake noticed a change in Matisse's demeanour after she spent the day with him and Mel's kids. Sure, she was still wary of him but at least she didn't back-pedal furiously every time he overstepped her "boundary marker"—intentionally or otherwise.

She even allowed him to view the current canvas she was painting. He knew this was a privilege and didn't treat it lightly. The table was strewn with tubes of paint, brushes, rags, sponges and various containers. Under the paint-splattered wooden easel, the drop cloth was likewise covered with splodges of colour.

Jacob was surprised that she stood nervously to the side fiddling with a paintbrush while he studied the work in progress. There was a photo of a stand of manna gums clipped to the top of the frame that she was using for reference. He recognised the spot from along the road down towards the Lightstation. The extra-large painting was probably three-quarters finished. He took a couple of steps back and folded his arms as the trees appeared seemingly from nowhere, complete with a koala or two in the branches. He treated her work with the reverence it deserved.

"You have an amazing gift, Matisse. This is good ... no, it's not just good ... it's incredibly good." Jacob heard her exhale as if she'd been holding her breath waiting for him to pass judgement. He glanced over at her, but her eyes were fixed on the painting.

She walked in front of him to the table, picked up the palette and dipped the brush into some dark brown paint. Jacob thought she would probably call it burnt umber or some such thing. She added a couple of strokes to the middle of the right-hand side, and stood back just near him, contemplating her next brush stroke. He knew she wasn't intentionally ignoring him; she was just immersed in what she was painting.

He looked around at the other canvases leaning up against the wall. There was a second easel in the corner. Jacob moved closer to have a better look at the large canvas it held. He'd seen glimpses of it on other occasions. There was a series of head and shoulder silhouettes, six across and the same number down the canvas, painted in a variety of colours but mostly black. The first couple of silhouettes were painted in vibrant colours and then black. Rows of black. The last two or three painted figures though held a hint of light and colour just at one edge. The bottom row and a half were still at the pencil stage.

Matisse came over to where he was standing,

"It's a representation of what I have been going through over the last couple of years, but obviously, it's not finished yet." She pointedly turned the painting over and walked back to the other easel.

He took the hint and went back to work.

JACOB INVENTED some flimsy excuse when he got back from his latest trip to call around and see his sister. Actually, it was just to see Matisse. He knew she was staying at the motel for a couple of days. As he drove his Ranger into the carpark, he noticed a couple walking towards a silver hire car. They had their arms around each other, and her head was inclined towards something he was saying. The first thing he noticed was the apparent age difference between the pair.

Then he realised the woman was Matisse.

She hugged the older man and kissed him briefly before waving him off. Jacob clenched his teeth, and the muscles in his arms tightened as he felt a surge of something, rising up inside him. He wasn't about to admit it was jealousy. Matisse would have noticed his Ranger, so there was no use pretending he hadn't seen her. She was almost level with his car door by the time he turned off the engine and got out.

"Hi Jacob, back from your trip already?" She didn't seem the least bit embarrassed.

"Hello Matisse, how are you going today?"

"Yeah, good thanks."

He had to know. "So, was that a friend of yours?"

But Matisse seemed unconcerned. "Oh, that was Max. He's my agent. He just needed to come and see for himself that I'm still alive."

Sure, he did, Jacob thought. But he didn't say it out loud. "So, what are you up to?"

"I've got to go to the post office. There's a canvas shipment that's arrived for me."

"Jump in, I'll take you."

"You sure it's not too much trouble?"

"Not at all."

"Oh, okay then." Opening the door, she climbed up beside him.

Jacob tapped his frustration out on the steering wheel as he drove, making a few offhand responses to her interest in his trip. He knew he had no right to question her about Max or whatever his name was, but still ... he saw what he saw, and he didn't like it one little bit.

Every carpark space near the post office seemed to be taken, so Jacob had to stop quite a distance away. As he walked alongside her, he seemed to be saying hello to someone every ten metres.

"You're popular," she observed, after he stopped to chat to someone for the umpteenth time.

"Our family has been connected to this town for generations, so I guess most people know who I am." He didn't add that his family probably provided employment for a significant number of the town's population through the various businesses they owned.

MATISSE DIDN'T KNOW whether to stop and wait or keep walking when Jake excused himself and jogged across the road to speak to an older lady. He bent down and listened to what she was saying and then picked up her grocery bags and carried them to her small white sedan. Matisse waited a couple of minutes and then started walking. Jacob soon caught up with her.

"Mrs Byers has known me since I was a baby," he said. "She was my Year 2 teacher and also taught both my sisters. But she'd given it up by the time Todd was ready for school, after her late husband was diagnosed with cancer. She was a total legend around here. Parents fought to get their kids into her class."

In a few more steps, he stopped again, "Do you mind if I duck into the office for a moment?" He indicated a shopfront she'd not noticed before. Great Ocean Touring. She hesitated, unsure if she should follow, until he stopped and held the door open, gesturing for her to go ahead of him.

The first thing that she noticed was a huge aerial shot obviously taken over the coastal road dominating the wall. All three of the female staff behind the counter lit up when they saw Jacob walk in. Matisse saw their reactions and felt annoyed. Why? She had no idea—or did she? Maybe it was that they seemed to be enamoured with him. Oh no—she couldn't possibly be a little bit jealous. Could she?

Jacob introduced her to each of the women in turn. They seemed friendly enough towards her. She pretended to be distracted by the wall to her left, filled with stunning photos of the Twelve Apostles and other local landmarks, as well as numerous framed awards. There was an amazing sunset photo that drew her. Glancing at Jacob, who seemed to be signing a bunch of paperwork while joking with the women, she kept studying the wall intently.

"So, do you work for Great Ocean Touring?" she asked, once they were back outside.

"You could say that," he said, and paused for a minute. "Actually, it's my business," he admitted.

"Oh, really? So what sort of touring do you do?"

"Walking tours of the Great Ocean Road mostly—anywhere between three and seven days."

"That sounds great. I imagine they are popular?"

"Yes, as a matter of fact it's growing every year, which is fantastic." He didn't elaborate, so she didn't press him further. Now she thought of it there was one photo on the wall of a group of people trekking—the guide was probably Jacob. Maybe she should think about doing a walk herself—it would give her another painting perspective. That sunset photo she'd been drawn to was spectacular.

As she signed for her parcel at the post office, she was glad to have Jacob to manhandle it. Better still, he offered to deliver it out to the cabin.

JACOB HAD A FAVOUR TO ASK. As soon as Charlie saw Matisse, he bounded over and slid in sideways, hitting his rump on her legs, expecting a pat. He wasn't disappointed.

"I was wondering if you would mind looking after Charlie

for me while I'm away. I'm running late, and it would save me taking him to my folks. He seems to like you." *Okay, it would give me a convenient reason to return.*

"Sure, I would love to look after Charlie." She rubbed the dog's back. "You wanna stay here for a holiday, boy?"

Jacob brought in food for his dog and other bits and pieces. Charlie seemed totally unconcerned. "Thanks Matisse. I'll be back in about ten days."

"No problems, see you then."

Jacob bent down to pat the dog and told him to behave while he was gone.

CHARLIE NEVER SEEMED to miss his owner one bit. He lapped up all the attention Matisse lavished on him. He slept by the back door, but didn't hesitate to come in and disturb her if he thought she should be awake. There was an early morning walk and another in the afternoon.

In between times, she painted and painted, often forgetting to eat—or sleep, for that matter. She knew Max would be horrified, but she felt exhilarated more than tired. The stack of finished canvases grew rapidly, maybe because her biggest distraction, Jacob, wasn't around, so her focus was more intentional.

When Matisse took her regular drive into town, Charlie went along for the ride, happy to hang his head out of the side window of the van. She tied him up in the shade near her vehicle, with some water, while she went in to replenish her supplies at the grocery store. After picking up her mail, Matisse drove to the Bay View Motel and called into the gallery.

"Hi, I didn't expect to see you," Melanie told her.

"I'm not staying. I'm on a bit of a roll at the moment, so I don't want to get distracted. Even coming into town is a bit of a risk." She handed a sizable package to Melanie. "Here are a few more paintings for you."

"Good! The other ones flew off the shelf. I'll easily sell whatever you can give me. And another thing." Mel paused. "We're always on the lookout for ways to raise money for the State Emergency Service and, well, I wondered if you might consent to allowing us to sell some limited edition prints of your work. I'm sure they would be well received."

Matisse nodded thoughtfully. "Yes, I don't see why not. I could come up with a couple of images and donate them."

"I was thinking along the lines of greeting cards and notebooks and maybe coffee mugs?"

"As long as it doesn't run to tea towels and oven mitts," she joked.

"No, I wouldn't dream of it. You would have the final say in what was produced."

They talked for a bit before Matisse heard Charlie barking. "Oh crumbs, I'd better go. See you around."

Melanie walked with her friend out to the van, obviously surprised to see her brother's dog in the passenger seat with his head out the window. She walked over to pat him. "Hey Charlie, what are you doing here?"

"Jacob asked me to mind him while he was away."

"Really? Well that's a pretty big compliment."

"Oh? Why is that?"

"Jacob won't let just anyone mind his dog. Usually Mum and Dad get the job. He must think a lot of you to entrust Charlie to your care."

Matisse shrugged.

"No, seriously Matisse. It's a big deal."

"If you say so ... I'd best get going now. Bye." Matisse climbed into the driver's seat and gave Charlie a pat. "C'mon, boy, let's go."

She mulled over Melanie's words as she headed back to the cabin. Did Jacob think a lot of her? She didn't rightly know.

They were getting along better. She kept her distance—not to the same extent admittedly—but he still threw her off balance every time he was around.

~

"I've been reading up on that Australian artist you've been compared to. What's his name, Russell ...?"

"John Russell."

Jacob had arrived to pick up Charlie, and found the dog with Matisse in her spot down by the creek.

"You have to admit he's got an interesting story though, hasn't he?" Jacob commented as he sat down next to her.

"I guess so. It's pretty amazing to think that he was a friend of Van Gogh and Monet, but unlike them he never received the acclaim he deserved. Especially as the others in their group, including the likes of Rodin and Henri Matisse, claimed they learnt so much from him."

"I saw that he was pretty distraught after losing his wife and supposedly destroyed 400 or more paintings and ..." he trailed off, not looking at her.

"And your point is?"

"I know you don't like the comparisons, but I just wondered if there were any parallels by any chance. Did you destroy any of your work after the accident?"

She had provided him only sketchy details about Jonno and the accident. Her answer was quiet.

"As a matter of fact, I did," she admitted. "Not quite as many, though. Thankfully Max had visited a month or so before the accident and taken most of the canvases back to Sydney with him. After I got out of hospital and we eventually went back to Bali, to the villa, Max made the mistake of leaving me alone. The grief and anger just overtook me, and I went a bit crazy. If he hadn't come back when he did, I may well have destroyed the place ... At a guess, I'd say less than a dozen got wrecked, including the ones I had painted of Jonno."

Jacob noticed she was holding the pendant she wore around her neck, sliding it back and forth on the chain. He reached out and hooked his finger under it. There was a surfboard and wave engraved on the front. "You play with this a lot."

"Do I? I hadn't really noticed."

"It obviously means a lot to you. Was it a gift from him?"

She looked down at the disc in his fingers. "Close," she told him as Jacob let the pendant drop. "Jonno always wore it. When his family went to pack up his belongings, they missed it." She took the pendant in her paint-stained hand. "The chain had broken, and he wasn't wearing it at the time of ..." She trailed off. "Anyway, when Max and I were moving my stuff, I found it and got a new chain. It's about all I have of him."

"What about your engagement ring?"

"To be honest, it was just a painful reminder of that night, so I sold it and the money went to the hospital where I was first treated. I went back to thank the doctor who saved my life. To cut a long story short, some of the proceeds from the sale of my artwork goes to support the school in the doctor's home village, as well as the hospital."

"I'm impressed. Good on you."

She shrugged. "I just wanted to show my gratitude in a practical, ongoing way, and it gives me something to focus on if I'm having a bad day. I remember all the schoolchildren I'm supporting, and that helps keep me going."

While she was being talkative, he decided to see if she'd open up a bit more. "So, tell me about Jonno," he ventured.

She glanced at him, apparently surprised at the statement. "There's not much to tell." Bang. He could practically hear the wall fly back up.

"I met Jonathan when he came to Bali on a surfing holiday. He was supposed to go back and start work in the family transport and logistics company, but he stayed with me instead because we were in love. It didn't go down too well with his family. We went out to dinner. I was pillion passenger on the scooter. It crashed.

"I survived. He didn't. That will be two years ago on the twenty-third of this month, and I miss him every moment of every day."

With that she got up and walked, and kept walking downstream, away from the cabin and Jacob.

He let out a slow breath and watched her go. He wasn't sure if any gains that had been made in their relationship had just been wiped out—he hoped not. Only time would tell.

CHAPTER EIGHT

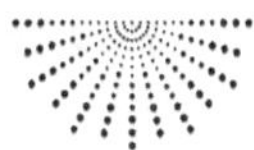

*J*acob was taking notes where he stood. The informal board meeting included the Davis family plus the extras who served alongside, gathered around the dining room table at his parents' place. The meeting was just winding up and discussion had turned to the following day's staff social barbecue lunch.

"Oh, and by the way, I've invited a friend to come along and be the official photographer. I thought it might be nice to get some family photos taken for whoever wants them." He was met with approval.

"It wouldn't be that girl you've got holed up down by the creek by any chance, would it?"

Trust you, Todd, Jacob thought, wishing not for the first time that his younger brother had stayed overseas. "Yes, as a matter of fact, Matisse is coming to take photos for us."

"Is this a paying job or as a volunteer?"

"I believe she's doing it because I asked her, nicely."

"Are you sure she's not just angling after the family fortune … or at least yours, bro?"

"As far as I know she doesn't know anything about that, and I'd prefer to keep it that way for as long as possible."

"Sure, she doesn't." Todd was on a roll and apparently intended to keep it up for a while longer, to stir his older brother. He kept at him.

Eventually, Jacob tired of it all and went to leave the room.

Todd had one last parting shot. "Hey Jacob, is she a friend with benefits?"

"Knock it off, Todd," his father warned.

"I'd appreciate it if he could be kept on a short leash tomorrow," Jacob muttered as he pushed the door open a little harder than intended.

MATISSE PULLED her thick hair back into a ponytail, and then pulled it out again. Shaking it out, she bent forward then flicked it back, sweeping it to the right side, looking at it critically in the small mirror hanging from the nail beside the bedroom door. Screwing her nose up, she undid that style as well.

"Stop being ridiculous," she scolded herself, "no one will really care about your hairstyle."

But she cared. She was more than a little nervous about the day ahead, meeting the rest of the Davis family. She should never have agreed to go—but she was curious to meet the rest of the clan. Melanie had quickly become a friend. She got on well with Adam and the kids. As for Jacob, well she was not entirely sure what she thought of him. She found herself attracted to him. Maybe because he was so different to her late fiancé. Tall and dark compared with Jonno's typical blond surfer-boy look.

There was nothing typical about Jacob Davis, however, and certainly no comparison. Every day he was pulling her in, ever so slowly. Maybe it was like the story of the frog in hot water. Put him in a pot of hot water and he'd jump out straight away—but put the frog in regular water and turn the heat up slowly, the frog adjusts and never knows what has hit him until too late.

She sighed—was that the truth? Was Jacob turning the heat

up on their relationship so slowly she hardly noticed? Then wham—it would hit her with a rush, and it would be too late to pull back. But now she was aware, did she want to do anything or just see what happened?

Eventually, she made some tiny braids on either side of her head and pulled the ends back with the rest of her hair into a messy bun.

Matisse gathered her camera gear and set it out on the front veranda at the top of the stairs. She'd spent ages trying to figure out what to wear. Not that there was a whole lot to choose from. Something casual but a little dressy. The jeans and the low-heeled tan boots were the easy part. Then Matisse decided on a white t-shirt, teaming that with what she called her "Impressionist" top. It wasn't quite a kaftan, but it didn't have the structure of a jacket. There were long, loose sleeves fitted at the wrist and it flowed down mid-thigh. It looked like a piece of artwork. An eye-catching riot of colour that blended from reds to yellow, green and blue. A spring garden perhaps. She'd had it for many years. It was beautiful, and made her feel brighter than she was feeling.

Hearing the four-wheel drive pull up, she headed outside, hoisted the camera bag onto her shoulder and walked to where Jacob stood waiting with the car door open. He was also wearing jeans with a dressier pair of RM Williams boots. The top button of his blue chambray shirt was open, the long sleeves rolled up mid-arm.

"Thanks for coming. I really appreciate you doing this."

"You'd better wait until you see the results before you thank me," she told him, slipping into her seatbelt. He put his arm across the top of the seat behind her as he put the car into reverse. "So, who's going to be there?"

"Mum and Dad, obviously. Mel, Adam and the kids. My other sister Andrea, and Sam, and their three—Ben, almost ten, Luke, eight, and Molly, five." He changed gears and spun the steering wheel to drive forward. "Oh, and you will get to meet Todd."

"He's the youngest, right?"

"Yes, he's twenty-three. Just arrived two days ago from backpacking in Europe. He's probably run out of money and looking to top up his bank account before he disappears again. He's a bit full-on—so I'm just warning you ahead of time."

"Okay. I'll take that on board. And who else?"

"Well, there'll be any number of staff and their families. It's their end of year get-together. My parents host at least two functions a year. One here at home and the second at another property—they usually rotate it between Warrnambool, Ballarat or Bendigo. They make a weekend of it. Purely a social gathering— no business talk allowed."

"So, what did you have in mind for me to do?"

"I've staked out a spot I think will be suitable to do family photos for anyone who wants them. I'm hoping we can get all of the Davis family together for long enough as well. And any candid shots around the place would be great."

Jacob gave Matisse a family history lesson as they drove. "The house was built in the mid–1860s, not long after the telegraph station over at Cape Otway. My great-great grandparents purchased it in 1886 and named it Pembroke after John's birthplace in Wales. Interestingly, Pembroke, Wales, also has limestone formations along its coastline called The Green Bridge of Wales. Anyway, their son Jacob, after whom I'm named, was born in 1890. My grandfather, Luke, was born in the 1920s, and Dad in the mid–50s. It's been in the Davis family for almost a hundred and thirty years. Of course, it's been rewired, renovated, modernised and added to over that time."

Matisse was impressed. "So, what happens when your parents pass away?"

"It will still remain in the family. Andrea and Sam are gradually taking on more responsibility, although I'm not sure they will end up in the homestead. But there's plenty of time to decide that—my parents are both very fit and healthy, so I can't see them retiring anytime soon."

"Did you say your parents have other properties?"

Jacob paused. "Yes, well, there's one in the other towns I mentioned."

There was little more than a goat track between Jake's property and his parents', albeit a well-worn one that would save them having to drive the long way to the Lightstation road and around. Eventually, Jacob turned the Ranger onto a driveway that ran in both directions as far as Matisse could see. It was a long winding gravel affair lined with majestic trees, hedged sides and solar lighting running its length. The driveway swept around to the front of a low white veranda-fronted building. There was a garden bed out front with a three-tier circular fountain in the centre. Instead of taking the circular drive, Jacob drove down the right-hand side of the house to the rear, and parked in front of a triple garage built at a right angle to the house.

"It's very beautiful, Jacob."

"Yeah, it is, isn't it?"

"I don't suppose your parents have thought of hosting weddings here? The house and grounds out the front would make a perfect backdrop."

"As a matter of fact, they do, Matisse. Both my sisters were married here. There can be a marquee set up on the grassed area in front of the house alongside the drive. It looks pretty magical lit up at night, and it lends itself perfectly to having a horse and carriage. The Sinclairs next door have a carriage that gets used on occasions, along with their bush chapel. It's probably a ten-minute carriage ride from here." He grinned. "Our stables were converted to accommodation, so the bridal party can stay here, take the horse and carriage over to the chapel, then return for the reception."

"Do you mind if I ..."

"Have a look around? Sure. People aren't due to arrive for another hour or so, and knowing Mum and Andrea, they will have it all under control." He led her out to the front of the house.

She stepped up and stood on the corner of the veranda, absorbing the view. Beyond the driveway was a lush expanse of grass backed by a grove of trees. To the far right she could see a path heading off into the greenery. She had to stop herself from taking off to see where it led. Turning back, she noticed the front door was open. Matisse looked at Jacob.

"Go for it."

Stepping inside onto the deep, rich hardwood of the beautiful floor, Matisse could see through wide doorways either side of the broad entry hall and into the rooms beyond. On the left was what Jacob told her would have been a drawing room, connecting to the main bedroom and to the right, a lounge led into a formal dining room. Jacob said much of the furniture wasn't original, but replicated what may have been there a hundred years ago. The front rooms all contained fireplaces, but some of them had been modernised to run on gas. He demonstrated how the television and sound systems were cleverly hidden in furniture.

Matisse could easily picture family life here over the years. She followed Jacob further into the house. He stood back, and allowed her to walk through a bedroom door.

"This was originally my room until Todd came along, then I was relegated to the back out there," he said, pointing further down the hall. The "boys' room" had a huge four-poster bed and large wardrobe. The room his sisters had occupied next door was similarly furnished. The curtains on the French doors were tied back, revealing glimpses of the lush gardens to the side of the homestead. There was a step down at the back of the house where a section had been added. Jacob's old room was long and narrow and still contained the king single bed, a small desk, and wardrobe.

"Do visitors stay here in the main house?" she wanted to know.

"Not usually, although Mum and Dad will host dinner parties. Apart from the old stable, there's a cottage and some self-contained cabins further down, but you can't see them from here." By now they'd walked back through the well-appointed kitchen, all white and timber with gleaming appliances, a huge island bench to one end, and a mid-sized wooden table and chairs at the other.

"Everyone's outside. Come on."

The back of the homestead was bordered by the garage on one side and a similar building opposite which Jacob told her was the family games room. Matisse could see the old stables further back and a cottage to the right of that. The family was gathered around several tables with navy checked tablecloths, which stood ready to receive food the visitors would contribute. Chairs and bench seats dotted the area. Matisse walked over with Jacob to join them.

"This is my mum, Claire." He introduced Matisse to a tall, well-dressed woman in her early sixties who looked like she had just stepped out of a *Country Style* magazine.

She greeted Matisse warmly. "So nice to finally meet you." She kissed Matisse on the cheek.

"Hello, Matisse, glad you could make it." Jacob's father, James, likewise kissed her.

"I'm Andrea, Jake's older sister," the younger version of Claire Davis told her. Matisse greeted Andrea's husband, Sam, and thanked him again for helping Jacob and his dad to replace the cabin roof. Matisse hugged Mel and greeted Adam. Their kids were off somewhere with their cousins. Matisse was handed a drink and they chatted a while.

"I'll show you where I thought you could take the photos."

Leaving her empty glass on the table, Matisse followed Jacob to a spot in the garden on the far side. "I think it will work," she told him, glancing around.

"Great. I'll go get your gear."

"That's okay, I can go." He walked with her anyway.

They'd hardly got to the Ranger when a black convertible came roaring up behind them and pulled noisily alongside. The driver, dressed head to toe in black, pulled reflective sunglasses off his eyes and hung them from the vee of the button-down shirt that showed off his slim physique as he bounded out. There was no doubt he was Jacob's younger brother. A little shorter than Jacob, he had a similar build, but his eyes and hair were several shades lighter. Matisse wondered if this was how Jacob had looked at that age. The older Davis sibling had filled out and matured deliciously over the years.

Todd wasted no time introducing himself. "You must be the artist my big brother has been hiding down at the cabin. I'm the much-loved and much-spoiled baby of the family." He took her hand, brought it to his lips and kissed it slowly, and grinned at her mischievously.

"Hi Todd." She smiled back. He kept hold of her hand.

"When you are sick of hanging around old Jakey here, let me know, and I'll be happy to show you a much better time, okay Matisse?"

"I'll keep it in mind, thanks."

"Hey man." He slapped his brother on the back. "You're punching way above—just saying." He grabbed a couple of ice bags from the back of the sports car. "See you later, gorgeous." He blew a kiss to Matisse over his shoulder as he jogged off through the gateway between the house and garage.

"And that was Todd."

"So I gather."

"You are obviously on his radar now, so you'd better watch out. If his previous form is anything to go by, he'll be tailing you the rest of the day."

"Seriously?"

"'Fraid so."

"He's driving a pretty fancy car if he's low on funds."

"What can I say? Spoiled baby of the family, like he said. He probably just charged it to the business account."

Matisse set up the camera gear, and Jacob managed to gather the family for some photos. She quickly positioned everyone and got to work. Todd insisted on giving her a hard time, apparently saying anything half-smart he could think of to get a rise out of her.

He was doing a pretty good job of it.

"Adam, get your hands off my sister's butt."

"Matisse, why don't I help you with your photography? We can see if anything develops."

"Instead of cheese, let's all say 'sex'."

"Jeez, Andi and Sam. Get a room, for crying out loud—think of the children."

Matisse could feel the colour warming her cheeks as she tried to ignore him. He didn't take any notice of his mother's admonishments, or anyone else's for that matter. It just spurred him on. In the end, Matisse gave him back as good as he was dishing out.

"Can someone clip him over the ear for me?" she begged as she set up another shot.

Adam was standing next to him in the line-up. "My pleasure." He obliged.

As guests started to arrive, she hurriedly took head and shoulder shots of Jacob's parents so they could go and play hosts. Jacob was busy amusing his nephews and nieces, and Matisse managed to click off a couple of frames unnoticed. By the time she had finished with Andrea and Melanie's families, both Jacob and Todd had disappeared.

The aroma from the barbecue was making her mouth water as she worked solidly taking photos. There must have been upwards of eighty people, and most seemed keen to have photos taken. Jacob stopped by with a plate of food and a thirst quencher when she had a break.

"How's it going?"

"Keeping me busy." He stayed with her to make sure she ate something.

"So, what's going to be the best way to get the photos from you?"

"I can put them on a USB stick when I'm in town next week."

"I had hoped to get them sooner."

"No power where I am, remember. No juice for the laptop."

"Okay then, how about I run you past my place on the way home, and you can put them straight onto my computer?"

"That might be better."

He looked behind her as he reached for her empty plate. "Looks like you have some more customers."

WANDERING AROUND LATER TAKING candid photos, Matisse preferred the unguarded moments to the posed shots. As soon as she was able, she packed up and snuck away for a few minutes of peace and quiet to clear her head. There was a path between the stable and the cottages that led down towards a grove of trees. Matisse left the noise behind her, looking for a spot to relax. There was a run-down shed of some sort which she walked behind. Leaning back against the wall with her eyes closed, she breathed deeply. The serenity didn't last.

"There you are." Matisse didn't move.

"Whatcha doing, pretty lady?" *How much had he had to drink?*

"I was enjoying the quiet. What do you want, Todd?"

"I want you to run away to Europe with me." She looked at him. He was a little too close.

"I thought you were home because you'd run out of money."

He shrugged. "I'm sure my brother will loan me some to get me out of his hair. You have the most amazing eyes, but I'm sure Jacob has already told you that."

"I'm not your type, Todd."

"You can't know that for sure ... but it could be fun to find out." He reached out to touch her cheek, but she pushed his hand away.

"I can save you the effort. Why don't you go and chase someone your own age?" She crossed her arms across her chest.

"I'd rather enjoy chasing you, to be honest." He looked her up and down. "I've always looked up to my brother ... admired his taste in toys, clothes, cars and women. I often find myself wanting what he has."

"You can't always get what you want in life."

"Yes, but you forget I'm the spoiled baby and what Todd wants, Todd usually gets." He leaned in to kiss her with his beer-tinged breath, but she shoved him away.

"Not this time, mate."

"Come on Matisse, just one little kiss." He took a step closer.

"Back off, Todd."

"Saving yourself for my brother, are you?" he sneered.

"Okay, now you've overstepped the mark. Get out of here."

They faced off. She held her nerve. Todd blinked first. "Can't blame a guy for trying."

She slumped back against the shed wall as he strode away.

MEL MOTIONED TO JACOB. "Have you seen Matisse?"

"No, why?"

"Todd just came stalking through here. I wondered if he thought he'd try it on with her."

"Did you notice which way he came?"

Mel pointed down to the area behind the stables.

"I'll go and check it out." Jacob soon spotted Matisse near the old machinery shed and walked over.

"Hey."

She turned on him. "I thought I told you to get—" She stopped abruptly. "Oh, I thought you were ..."

"Todd," he finished for her. "I figured that. Sorry, he slipped his collar when I wasn't watching."

She managed a weak smile.

"Are you okay?"

She nodded.

"Did he try to …?"

Matisse was quick to reassure him. "He tried, but he didn't get very far."

Jacob clenched his fist.

"It's okay, Jacob, I'm fine really. He's just a brash young man. He's a bit full of it."

"Yeah, I know." He relaxed his hand.

"He idolises his brother, you know. Just wants what you have."

"Well, he could if he worked hard enough. I'm not about to hand him anything on a platter."

"You mean the spoiled baby won't get what he wants?"

"He needs to grow up a bit first."

"That might take a while."

Jacob agreed with her.

Matisse took his arm as they started to walk back. "Please tell me you weren't as obnoxious at his age?"

"No, I don't believe so, but you might like to check with my sisters for confirmation."

"You know he actually reminds me a lot of Jonno … not quite as much charm, though. One Jonno in my life is about all I can handle. I certainly don't need or want another."

She dropped her hand from his arm as they reached the old stables. He was surprised how keenly he felt the loss of her hand on his arm, her warmth.

~

"It was a near thing," Jacob told Melanie a few minutes later while Matisse went to retrieve her camera gear.

"She okay?"

"Yeah, just a little shaken up, but she put him in his place."

"Honestly, that boy," she muttered. That boy was already busy chatting up someone else as if nothing had happened. "He's got some nerve that brother of ours."

"He'll cop it one day if he's not careful."

"We can live in hope."

"Might teach him a lesson, hey." Jacob didn't leave Matisse's side for the rest of the afternoon, just in case. Todd never came anywhere near them.

CHAPTER NINE

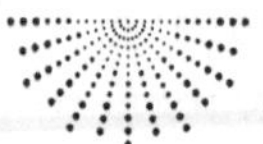

"You have your own helicopter?" Matisse asked incredulously, looking at the Davis Air insignia on the tail of the chopper as they pulled up outside his home.

"I have several, actually. Apart from the walking tours, my main business is running joy flights around the coastline. This one," he indicated, "is for the VIP clients, but I mostly use it myself because I travel a lot and it's quicker to fly to Avalon or Melbourne to catch a commercial flight than to drive."

Jacob led the way up the stairs to the main living area of his home. Matisse was automatically drawn to the large windows that dominated the room. Slipping the camera bag strap off her shoulder, she dropped the bag the last couple of centimetres to the floor and walked in awe across the large living area to take in the view. The expanse of Bass Strait before her was incredible. The tones of colour. Cerulean, turquoise, ultramarine, cyan—all blended together. Automatically, she was itching to paint the seascape. Jake opened the sliding door onto the balcony and handed her a pair of binoculars when she stepped out next to him.

"If you look over that way," he said pointing, "you can see

the lighthouse." She followed his outstretched arm and focused on the landmark.

"Oh yes, I can see it now. That's amazing, I think I can even make out some people up top." He leaned on the rail and watched her delight as she surveyed the view. She put the binoculars down. "How could you ever get tired of that view?"

"I don't," he told her. "You should see it when a storm rolls in. Now that's a sight to behold."

"It's not as windy out here as I thought it would be."

"I had the house designed to minimise that, but it can still get pretty blowy, don't worry."

Matisse put the binoculars back to her eyes, "You've built quite a way back from the cliff edge."

"Yeah, it's just for safety reasons. I have lost about half a metre of land on the far right there since I moved here." She looked up at him, concerned.

"Don't worry, this place is over-engineered. There's no way it will go anywhere."

"Is it possible to get down to the water from here?"

"Sure, would you like to see?"

"Could I?"

A combination of steps and walking trail led to the left from the house, which Matisse took slowly. She passed a "Private Property – No Trespassing" sign near the bottom, to discourage anyone who might venture along the beach. The steps ended short of the sand where the ground had been washed away. Jacob dropped down and reached up to take Matisse around the waist and swing her down beside him. He held her a little longer than he needed to.

"Ah, thanks." She looked up at him and those dark eyes, and froze for an instant before pulling herself out of his grasp, fighting the desire to stay right where she was, with strong hands around her.

"Sorry there's not much beach for you."

"You could've organised high tide a bit better," she teased.

"Yeah well. If I'd known you were coming, I would have," he told her with a smile.

Her heart was doing strange things. Thumping erratically. She was sure he would be able to hear the noise. All she could think was to brush past him to walk to a rocky outcrop nearby. Pushing through a gap, she put some space between them, if only for a moment or two to catch her breath.

THE SECOND JACOB automatically reached up to help her down off the steps, he knew it wasn't a good idea. All he wanted to do was hang on to her waist and pull her in against him, so he could feel what it would be like to have her in his arms. When she looked up at him, he had to swallow hard. He wanted desperately to lean down and kiss her.

He hesitated, unsure of her reaction. Matisse pulled away and he let her go very reluctantly. She seemed to drop her guard for a couple of seconds, then brushed past him.

JACOB WAS SLOWER FOLLOWING her than she expected, giving her longer to compose herself. When she had thought he was about to kiss her, she had panicked and pulled away. Why? Did she really want him to kiss her? She was confused. Torn.

It was getting late and the breeze was picking up, although she was pretty sure it wasn't the cool air that made her shiver. Finding a rock to sit on, she closed her eyes, trying to block him out and clear her mind, but it wasn't working. She was acutely aware of his presence. If he came closer, she might not be able to resist his advances. Did she even want to?

Jacob sat what he thought was a safe distance away. The breeze caught the edge of her jacket, billowing it out. Reaching up, she pulled her hair free of its bun and ran her fingers through it. The wind gently tousled it about her head. Her eyes were shut, and she looked so peaceful, so kissable.

He had to force himself to stay put. Clamp down on his desire to reach for her and pull her close. He looked out to sea and tried to change the direction of his thoughts. The business. What was on his list of jobs?

They sat in companionable silence until the water lapped at their feet and Jacob motioned for her to follow.

He pushed his hands firmly into his pockets to keep them from getting him into trouble as she walked next to him back along the cool sand.

Matisse pulled her hair back into a ponytail as if she knew he was struggling to keep his hands out of its thickness.

Going ahead, he jumped the gap onto the bottom step, then leaned down to grab her hand and pull her up next to him.

He used a bit too much force, she overbalanced, clutched at the air and crashed into him. His automatic response was to put his hand on her back and steady her. Momentarily she was up against his chest. He relished having her softness against him—if only briefly. He quickly inhaled the scent of her hair.

"Whoa, careful there, are you alright?" His eyes locked with hers. She looked startled.

"Um, yeah I think so." She pulled her gaze away and he let her go reluctantly.

As Matisse concentrated on climbing the stairs back up to the house, Jacob kept his eyes fixed on the middle of her back— no higher, and certainly no lower. The steps seemed difficult for her and she stopped to rest a few times, but he kept his hands to himself, not trusting himself if he went to her aid.

He cast his mind back over the day. Apart from the incident with Todd, he hoped she had enjoyed her time at Pembroke. Granted, she had been much too busy behind the camera to interact much with his family, but she still seemed to make a positive impression on them.

∼

"HELP yourself to whatever you can find if you are hungry. I'll just turn the computer on."

As Matisse grabbed a banana, she stopped to survey the timberwork in the kitchen, running her hand along its smoothness. Gorgeous. The floors, the cabinetry and the furniture all matched. She wondered what timber had been used. The sleek stainless steel appliances finished the look.

It took her a couple of minutes to find where she had dropped her camera bag—on the edge of a massive rug halfway across the polished floor of the living room. She'd been so focused on the spectacular view outside earlier that she failed to notice the interior of the house was equally spectacular. Turning around slowly, she took in the lounge to her far right with its comfortable-looking seating, and back to the dining area. For one person it was a pretty big home.

She could imagine herself on the lounge near the fireplace on a cold winter's night, sipping hot chocolate and snuggling up next to Jacob with a couple of little ones stretched out alongside. *Oh dear. Where did that come from?* Giving herself a mental shake, she bent to retrieve her bag and took the camera along the corridor.

"I'm in here," he called out, "second door on the left."

"Your place is amazing," she told him, leaning on the door frame as he bent over his desk.

"Thanks."

"That timber is ... divine. What sort is it?"

Jacob glanced up at her. "Mountain Ash—it's all from the property here. Remember the outdoor bench?" Matisse nodded at him. "Everything you see has been reclaimed from fallen trees."

"Oh, wow."

He motioned her to sit down. "I've set up a new folder. If you wouldn't mind putting the photos in there, that would be great." He clicked the mouse and straightened up. "I'll leave you to it."

Matisse pulled out a cable as Jacob left the room, connected her camera to the computer's USB port and waited for the photos to flick up onto the screen. As she scrolled through, choosing which ones to copy, she paused at some shots of Jacob with the younger family members, totally engrossed in the moment. Uncle Jacob was clearly adored. Her heart skipped a beat. He would make a terrific father someday.

Oh, my. There were a couple of candid shots of Jacob that, for reasons she couldn't quite put her finger on, she decided not to share—to keep just for herself. She watched as the screen told her the other photos were being copied to the new file. It was dark by the time Matisse flicked the camera off, and she went looking for Jacob. He was sitting on a large black leather recliner.

There was a lamp on nearby and a business magazine tossed on the glass-topped coffee table beside him.

"All done," she told him.

"Great. Thanks. Would you like to sit for a bit?"

She paused, unsure what to say. "Yes, I guess so."

Jacob appeared not to notice as she took a recliner nearby. His eyes were closed.

"It's been a long day." They were both quiet for a while. Matisse was trying unsuccessfully to relax. Although she chose to put some physical space between them, she was still on edge. He had an unidentifiable effect on her.

"Hungry?" he said.

"I am, as a matter of fact."

"I'll see what I can find. Do you want to come and give me a hand?"

Jacob whipped up a quick omelette and they were soon

settled back in the lounge. The timber armrests were set off by the black upholstery on the chairs. Matisse couldn't help running her hand over and over the timber as she tucked her feet underneath her. Jacob reached for a remote control. A television screen appeared from a cabinet across the room. He channel-surfed before settling on a travel documentary. Matisse put her plate down on the side table next to her. The seats were as soft and comfortable as they looked, and she was so tired.

IT HAD BEEN A LONG DAY, no wonder she was exhausted. Jacob couldn't help himself, watching her as she slept. Captivated. Everything about her pulled him in. The steady rise and fall of her chest, head tipped towards him on the chair. She had pulled her hair out of the ponytail, and it was all he could do not to reach out and brush it away from her face. He settled back in his chair as he waited for her to stir. Maybe he even dozed off as well.

The words were out before he realised what he was saying. "How about you have a sleepover?"

"Pardon?" Matisse asked, rousing herself.

"Well, it's really late. Why don't you enjoy a real bed for a change?" He watched her as her eyes widened in alarm.

"Don't worry, there's no ulterior motive. I have a couple of spare beds and you can lock the door if you like."

Jacob threw a towel down on the bed for her, along with one of his t-shirts.

"In case you want something to sleep in. Bathroom's down that way. See you in the morning."

MATISSE DEFINITELY ENJOYED THE SHOWER, but vaguely wondered if she'd done the right thing staying. She was restless, wandering around the room, stopping herself with a hand on the door. Wanting to turn the knob, knowing if she left the bedroom to find Jake it would alter things irrevocably between them. Walking away she came back to the door several times, put her hand out and pulled away at the last minute as if she had been scalded. In the end her loyalty to the memory of Jonno won out and she stayed in the room.

JACOB WAS wide-awake at his computer, looking at the photos from the day. He sorted the files, deciding which shots to have printed for staff Christmas gifts. He was impressed with the job Matisse had done. Her artistic eye obviously carried over to her photographic work.

He paused then clicked onto Google and typed in Matisse Reynolds. Scrolling past the basics he already knew, he found some article links that caught his attention.

"Up-and-coming Sydney artist Matisse Reynolds was severely injured in a motor scooter accident in Bali. She was a pillion passenger and the unnamed driver was killed."

Jacob figured that the driver was Jonno, whoever Jonno was, apart from being Matisse's fiancé.

There was a follow-up story. *"Artist Matisse Reynolds has been flown to the Royal Prince Alfred hospital in Sydney after surviving a fatal scooter accident in Bali in which the unnamed driver, believed to be a fellow Australian, was killed."*

He kept scrolling: exhibition details. He clicked on photo links to see some of her artwork and saw she'd been awarded a scholarship to study in France. While it was enlightening, it certainly raised more questions than it answered. He glanced at the time on the screen realising it was much later than he thought.

CHAPTER TEN

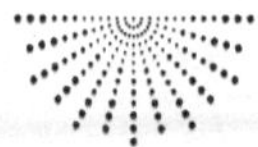

It took Matisse a minute or two to remember where she was. Jacob's house. Stretching her arms above her head as she glanced around, she realised she'd had a good night's sleep. Of course, the bedroom suite in this room was more of the same timber that was evident throughout the house. The bedhead was a heavy, solid piece of furniture.

Swinging her legs onto the floor rug, she spied the bedside clock, realising she'd slept in way later than usual. Her stomach growled as she padded to the bathroom. Keeping Jacob's t-shirt, she pulled her jeans on. The smell of freshly brewed coffee greeted her as she opened the door and found her way to the kitchen.

JACOB LOOKED over at the doorway. Matisse hadn't quite woken up. Barefoot, she ran a hand through sleep-tousled hair, pulling an elastic hair band from her wrist and in a couple of quick movements, secured her hair into a ponytail. He preferred it out.

"Good morning, how did you sleep?"

"Very well, once I actually got to sleep. It was such a full-on day; I was probably overtired."

"Coffee?"

"Yes please."

"How would you like it?"

"White with one thanks."

MATISSE PULLED out a black upholstered timber chair from the matching eight-seater table as he set a steaming mug before her.

She picked it up gratefully and inhaled the aroma. Much better than the instant she was used to having. Her host was barefoot, in jeans and a light blue t-shirt. She couldn't help but glance at him over the rim of her coffee mug, hoping it wasn't too obvious she was ogling. Wondering how long he'd been awake, she noticed he didn't have the rumpled, just rolled out of bed look she knew she was sporting. His hair was still damp from a shower and he'd shaved.

JACOB CROSSED his legs at the ankle as he leaned back on the bench with his own mug in hand. He had to admit to himself, he quite liked the idea of having her there in his kitchen ... in his life. He noticed she'd tied a knot on one side of the hem of his t-shirt she was wearing, to pull the size in a little. It looked way better on her he was sure. Matisse looked up and caught him out watching her. Shifting uncomfortably, he cleared his throat.

"I checked over the photos last night, thanks so much. There are some great ones there. I'll get some printed out for the staff, and there are a couple I will enlarge for my parents. It's not often we're in one place long enough."

"You're welcome, happy to help. I really like your family."

"What, even my baby brother?"

She screwed her nose up. "Okay, most of your family then ... Todd's not that bad I guess," she conceded.

"He's not always that good either."

She raised her mug in agreement, "He's not backward in coming forward, that's for sure."

Jacob changed the subject. "I was thinking pancakes for breakfast. You in?"

"Mmmm, yes please."

"With fresh orange juice?"

"Even better."

"But you are going to have to be responsible for that."

"Okay."

"Hand squeezed ..."

"Of course." He pulled out a timber cutting board along with a knife and set her up alongside him with a supply of cold oranges from the fridge. The pancake batter was already mixed, and he just had to heat up the pan. He pulled a roll of kitchen paper out along with a large white plate to hold the cooked pancakes.

They worked in easy companionability. As she finished squeezing the orange halves, she flipped them inside out and peeled the remaining flesh away to eat. There was some juice dripping down her chin and he had to fight the sudden urge to lick the sweetness off her face. Instead he pulled out a hand towel from the bottom drawer and gave it to her, not taking his eyes off her face as she wiped it clean. She caught him out again. He swallowed hard and cleared his throat.

"So, last night I took the opportunity to Google Matisse Reynolds."

"And what did you come up with?"

He knew he'd have to tread carefully here and avoided any mention of the accident. "Well, I can see now why they compare you to John Russell."

"The comparison is always flattering, but a little wide of the mark."

"Not from what I've seen of your work." He pulled a glass bottle of genuine maple syrup out of the pantry, and set it on the table along with some lemon wedges and strawberry coulis from the fridge.

"I don't know why I need to be pigeonholed as a female John Russell. Why can't I just be an original Matisse Reynolds? And anyway, were you stalking me?"

"No, I'd consider it more of a background check."

She laughed.

"So, you studied in Paris?" He added plates to the table along with cutlery.

"A long time ago. I received a scholarship for a three-month residency in a studio near Cité Internationale des Arts."

"Which is?"

"It's a non-profit international art centre. Provides studio accommodation for artists from around the world to come and study in Paris."

"Rent free?"

"I'm afraid not."

"Sounds like an amazing opportunity."

"It was. Have you ever been to Paris?"

"Oui, j'ai été à Paris." He shrugged. "I'm not a big fan of Paris to be honest, but I have business interests in New Caledonia, so I've picked up a bit over the years." They traded a few phrases in French.

Matisse grinned. "Your French is about as good as mine." She proceeded to tell him some anecdotes of her life in Paris. Becoming delightfully animated, she admitted visiting Montmartre to watch the artists at work every chance she could, and had amassed a sizable collection of their artwork. She said she never tired of watching the sun set over the city from the steps of nearby Sacré-Coeur Basilica, despite the inevitable throng of tourists. Jacob enjoyed listening to her. She had dropped her guard and was quite relaxed around him for a change. The stack of pancakes grew as he tried to keep the conversation going.

There was some gentle teasing in there which she didn't appear to mind, and sent a few zingers back his way.

"You must have adored all the galleries in Paris?"

"Oui."

"Did you get to Giverny?" he asked. Matisse rolled her eyes at him.

"You are seriously asking me, a so-called 'Impressionist artist', whether I've been to visit Monet's garden? Really?"

It was his turn to laugh. "Okay, that was obviously a ridiculous question. What I should have said was how many times did you go to Giverny?"

"Three times," she told him. "Have you been there?"

"Yes, as a matter of fact, I have." He thought a minute. "That bridge must be the most painted around."

She nodded. "I also managed to get to Belle Île as well." She didn't seem surprised by his blank look. "It's off the coast of Brittany. John Russell lived there for many years and established an artists' colony. It was amazing to be able to stand on that rugged coastline and see the places that feature in his paintings."

"Is that why you seem to have an affinity with the coastline around here?"

"Probably. I love Bondi, don't get me wrong, but the area around here has more appeal. I guess because it's not as populated."

"I know what you mean. That's why I enjoy living here at the bottom of the mainland. Anytime you want, feel free to come and get some inspiration."

"Thanks, I think I'd like that."

"So, would you go back to Paris?"

"In a heartbeat, but I know it's not for everyone."

"Touts everywhere you go—especially around the base of the Eiffel Tower," Jacob scowled.

"I think the good outweighs the bad."

Unless Jacob was mistaken, he thought he heard a car pulling up outside. There was no telltale bark from Charlie, so he suspected he knew who it might be. *Damn your timing.* To his mind, the noise of the key in the lock echoed loudly up the stairs. But if Matisse noticed she didn't say anything. The stairs were taken several at a time.

"Hey, smells like I'm in time for break ..." Todd trailed off at the sight of Matisse in the kitchen with his brother, stopping him in his tracks. Matisse didn't look up. Jacob shot Todd a warning glance, already regretting offering him a place to crash while he was back in the country.

~

"Fancy seeing you here, Matisse."

"Hi Todd."

He wandered over to the bench and picked himself an apple from the bowl close to where she was standing. He took a bite before looking at her thoughtfully.

"You look a bit tired there, Matisse. Didn't get much sleep last night, huh?"

Matisse coloured at his innuendo, while resisting the urge to slug his smug face. She knew exactly what he was getting at.

"Man, look at all this food. You must be ravenous this morning. All that horizontal exercise, no doubt."

Matisse wasn't about to rise to his baiting. She shot him a withering look. But he just smiled innocently at her. She could sense that Jacob was as annoyed as she was, barely holding back.

"So how do you like my brother's place?" he asked. "Pretty impressive isn't it?"

"It's okay," she was noncommittal.

"The view from the master bedroom is probably the best in the whole house I'd say."

"Really?" Matisse struggled to keep her voice even.

"Yep, surely you noticed yourself ... or maybe you were too preoccupied to give a damn."

"Coffee's ready, Todd. Would you like some?" She tried to change the subject.

Todd made a few more off-colour remarks before Matisse snapped and let him have it.

"Listen Todd, what your brother and I may or may not be doing is frankly none of your business. Enough of the smutty comments. Shut up or you can leave."

JACOB WAS IMPRESSED.

"Ouch," was Todd's only comment as he sat down and helped himself to the pancakes.

The chatty, relaxed Matisse disappeared as Jacob tried to steer the conversation into safer territory. As soon as Matisse had eaten, she asked Jacob to drop her back to the cabin.

"Sure thing." He pushed his chair away from the table and grabbed his keys on the way down the stairs. "You're on dish duty," he told Todd.

JACOB STOOD at the edge of the creek and looked back at the cabin. The renovations were coming along. Slowly. But that was a deliberate choice he had made in order to spend more time with Matisse. His frequent flyer points had taken a hammering, as work travel suddenly became less and less appealing.

Matisse came and joined him. She'd changed into one of the loose-fitting long-sleeved hippie type blouses she favoured. This one was the colour of butter.

She handed over his t-shirt. "I'd offer to wash it for you, but there's no machine." His fingers brushed hers as he took the offered shirt. He almost lifted it to his face to see if he could catch any trace of her perfume, but caught himself just in time.

She didn't move away. Jacob was close enough to see if she

would allow him to kiss her. He leaned down towards her, narrowing in on her lips. Almost ... at least she hesitated for a second.

He didn't try to stop her when she fled to the bench seat by the water. Jacob stood watching her sit there while he took a few deep breaths to steady himself ... and to let her have a few moments on her own. He walked over to where she was sitting.

Matisse wiped her eyes with one hand. "I'm sorry, Jacob, I'm not ready yet. I want to be ... but ... I'm not," she faltered.

He balled the t-shirt up in his hands, searching for the right words.

"I know Jonathan was the love of your life, and I don't want to diminish that in any way. But Matisse, one day I hope you'll realise you have the capacity to enjoy another relationship ... maybe even fall in love again ..."

He watched as she swallowed hard. "I'm scared, Jacob ... I don't think I could cope if I fell in love again with ... anyone ... and had to run the risk of losing them like I did with Jonno."

"Surely it's better to love and have lost than not to have loved at all?" He groaned inwardly at the hackneyed phrase.

"I'm ... not convinced ... at the moment." Her head was down, watching as she scuffed a shoe on the ground.

"Look, I'm prepared to be friends for the time being, but I won't keep it a secret that I'd like our relationship to be much more." Her foot stopped, but she didn't look up. "I can wait. I promise I won't make a move unless you feel you are ready. Okay?" There was a small nod. The best thing to do was to leave her for a while and give her some head space.

MATISSE HEARD THE CAR ENGINE. Then the tears came. She couldn't understand why she had turned down the offered kiss. She wanted it—oh how she wanted to feel his lips against her own. It had been a long time since ...

Shaking her head, she tried to get the image of Jacob out of her head—the tender look he gave her just as he bent towards her, the flash of disappointment when she backed away. He wasn't the only one disappointed by her actions.

Miserable, she trudged back to the cabin and headed for her artwork. Needing a distraction, she pulled another blank canvas from the pile and switched it out with the one on the easel. The ocean view from the clifftop at Jacob's house begged to be painted. All those beautiful shades of blue. She hadn't taken photos for reference, but she didn't need to—the scene was vividly locked away in her mind.

So was the vision of Jacob. Everything he did replayed on a continuous loop in her head, as much as she tried to push him out.

JACOB SLAMMED a few doors when he got back, annoyed with himself for making any admission about how he felt and for not realising that she wasn't ready. He'd probably have to start over and win her trust again.

"What's wrong with you, mate?" Todd asked. "Did you two have a fight?"

"None of your business."

"Sorry, did I arrive at the wrong time?"

"You could say that."

"Ruined your carnal plans for the day, huh?"

"Shut up, Todd."

"I might just have to go and console her then," he suggested.

Jacob's head snapped up. "If I find out you have been anywhere near Matisse, I'll ..."

"You'll what?" Todd challenged.

"Let's just say that Cain and Abel will have nothing on us, believe me." And at that moment he meant it.

CHAPTER ELEVEN

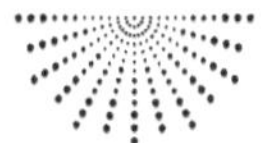

 acob had marked the date on his desk calendar weeks ago. "Double A Day" he'd dubbed it. Accident Anniversary Day. He wasn't quite sure how to approach it—he only knew Matisse shouldn't be by herself. Over the last few days, she had been gradually distancing herself. He hoped he might be able to distract her a little, so she didn't fall into a black hole.

He cancelled a business trip to be there. Armed with a large bunch of Australian wildflowers and a picnic basket he took off down to the cabin thinking if he got there early, he might be able to head things off at the pass. The cabin was quiet when he arrived. He walked cautiously around the back, but there was no sign of Matisse. The back door was ajar, so he dropped the picnic basket inside and found a container for the flowers and left them on the table. Hands in pockets, he stood on the back veranda.

A sudden overwhelming sense of dread punched him. *She wouldn't have ... would she?* Jacob launched himself down the stairs and almost ran to the creek. He hesitated, before remembering she usually walked downstream. Sending Charlie on ahead, he tried to fight a rising sense of panic.

He must've run a good two or three minutes before he

"

spotted her denim overalls and white tank top. A huge wave of relief washed over him. Her head and shoulders were down as she walked. He pulled up short, not wanting her to know he was worried.

As Charlie reached her, Matisse dropped to her knees and hugged him tightly. Her hair was loose and a bit dishevelled. Jacob slowed his walk. When he caught up, he got down on her level, keeping the dog between them. She was red-eyed from crying. It was all he could do to keep himself from pulling her into his arms there and then.

"Thought you could use some company today."

"I'm not going to be much fun to be around, sorry." Her lips trembled as she kept her eyes on Charlie, rubbing his head and down his back, in enough turmoil as it was without Jacob adding to it.

She stood and started walking slowly towards the cabin, eyes on the ground in front of her. Grief threatened to totally overwhelm her. It was as intense and raw as it had ever been. She had never expected to still be in such pain, and was embarrassed to be caught out by Jacob, of all people. She didn't want anyone, least of all him, to see her in such a mess.

Jacob fell in step beside her. Close, but not touching her. He didn't try to talk to her, to cheer her up. He just stayed on one side of her and Charlie on the other. Maybe it was good that he was here. No it wasn't. Her brain couldn't decide. When the tears started streaming again, she took the proffered handkerchief and pressed it hard against her eyes in a futile attempt to halt the flow.

If Jacob could have taken away the pain for her, he would

have. He struggled to see her hurting so much and knowing there was little in that moment he could do to ease her grief. He hoped that being there was of some small comfort.

As they neared the cabin, Matisse stopped under one of the manna gums by the water. She leaned back and slid down the trunk to the ground. Charlie automatically crouched down and put his head on her lap.

Jacob maintained a respectful distance, but close enough to keep a watchful eye on Matisse. He had some work he could go on with, to give himself something to do while she grieved.

SHE STROKED THE DOG, her thoughts a long way away. Matisse fingered the pendant around her neck, sliding it back and forth as she often did. What was it with all the tears? She thought she'd been healing, and then she'd get blindsided by a wave of grief. *Damn you, Jonno Reid.*

Matisse barely acknowledged Jacob's presence when he brought her some food at lunchtime. She ate on autopilot, and may as well have been eating cardboard for all she noticed or cared.

As JACOB SAT on the ground nearby, he felt a pang of ... what was it? Jealousy, perhaps, that Jonno still had a hold of her even two years later. That she wasn't able to see that there was someone else right next to her who cared a great deal about her. He had thought maybe, given enough time, she might come to care for him as well. But at that moment he doubted if she would ever be able to love another man with the intensity that she undoubtedly still loved Jonno. He tried to shake off his fears and convince himself that all she needed was time and patience.

Matisse hugged her knees up to her chest and put her head

down. Her hair fell forward, covering her face. He reached over to put a comforting hand on her shoulder, but she completely lost it. He pulled her into his arms and held her against his chest as she sobbed it out. There weren't any words he could use to console her. Instead he just stroked her hair and gently rubbed her back, murmuring what he hoped were words of comfort.

EVENTUALLY, Matisse realised where she was. The scent of fresh-cut timber registered with her, mingled with soap and just a vague hint of sweat. Jacob's calm and quiet strength had infused her with a growing sense of peace. She felt comforted sitting there with his arms wrapped around her. Comforted but not comfortable.

Aware that she was sitting on twigs and stones, Matisse became restless and sat upright. Jacob still had a hand on the back of her head, running his hand slowly down her hair.

"You okay?"

She nodded hesitantly. Matisse couldn't look him in the eye, and focused on his blue shirt, damp from her tears. "Um. Sorry to do that to you."

"Hey, anytime you need a shirt to cry on, let me know and I'll be there."

"Thanks," she sniffed. Matisse scrambled to her feet and Jacob followed. He kept a hand under her elbow as she swayed a little.

"I THINK I'll be right now," she whispered and took a small step away as he dropped his hand. She keenly felt the loss of the physical connection, and seriously contemplated changing her mind just so he would hold her again and she could melt into his arms.

"How about I leave Charlie with you?"

She nodded.

He picked up the picnic basket on the way back to the four-wheel drive. "Stay, Charlie, good boy."

Matisse got down and hugged the dog as Jacob backed the Ranger out and headed for home. But as soon as Matisse saw the flowers on the table, she burst into tears again.

CHAPTER TWELVE

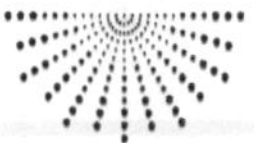

$\mathcal{A}$s usual, it was quiet when Jacob walked in the front door at Melanie's. He waited until Miss Lily chose to reveal herself. Pretending to be surprised when she ran at him, he scooped her up in her pink pyjamas.

"Uncle Jake!"

"Hello, gorgeous girl, how are you tonight?"

She wrapped her arms around his neck and hugged him fiercely. "Ex-cell-ent," she said, smothering him in kisses.

He laughed and set her down. "Where's your brother?"

"Computer," she told him, and darted off.

Jacob wandered into the kitchen.

"Hey Mel, you're looking hot tonight." His sister was wearing a little black fitted dress. She was distracted and hardly heard him.

"Yeah thanks, there's tacos for dinner and some popcorn if you do a movie. I know there's no school tomorrow, but can you try to have them in bed at a reasonable hour? Like eight at the latest for Lily and eight-thirty for Ashton?"

"Yes sir," he replied, giving her a mock salute.

She bustled around straightening things until Adam stopped

her. "Come on, hon, we'll be late." Mel went to say goodbye to Aston and Lily.

"Hey Jake, how's it going?"

"Yeah, okay."

"How are the cabin renovations coming along?"

"Slowly."

"That's not like you, Jacob. Thought you would have had it done by now. Bit distracted, are you?"

"Let's just say I'm in no particular hurry to finish."

"How's Matisse?"

"She has good and bad days I guess, sometimes it's hard to tell." He wasn't about to discuss the accident anniversary with Adam. "Then, some days, she gets so focused on her painting she's oblivious to anything else—or should I say, anyone else."

"She must be the only female who doesn't notice you."

"Sure, Adam."

"Sure what?" asked Mel, returning with her handbag and dropping it on the bench.

"Your brother's ego is dented because his artist friend gets so engrossed in her artwork, she hardly knows he's alive," Adam joked. She raised an eyebrow at them.

"I'm pretty sure she notices."

Adam pulled her into an embrace. "You got some inside information?" he asked kissing her.

"Wouldn't you like to know."

They were lost for a minute or two. Jacob envied their relationship. Actually, both of his sisters had found amazing life partners. He could only hope one day to join them. Adam and Sam had become firm friends, and he looked forward to their rare boys' weekends away.

"Ew, gross," Ashton commented as he came into the room and saw his parents kissing.

"I agree, mate," Jake told his nephew, ruffling his hair. "What are we playing tonight?"

"No more than an hour, Ashton," his father warned him,

fully aware that his brother-in-law would string things out beyond the time limit. That was his privilege as uncle.

"Yeah, Dad," he held up his hand for a high-five.

"Bye Lily," he called to his youngest. She appeared in the doorway.

"Bye Daddy. You look very handsome tonight." He wore black trousers and an open neck red shirt with the sleeves rolled up.

"Why thank you, m'lady." He got down on her level for a hug and a kiss. "Okay guys, behave for Uncle Jake, he's in charge now. I don't want to hear any bad reports when I get back." Ashton and Lily waved their parents off before turning to their adored uncle.

"Righto, what's first?" he asked the pair. Ashton and Lily looked at each other.

"Ticklefest!" they shouted together, and took off with their uncle in hot pursuit.

There was an intense amount of scruffing, noise, scrambling, tickling, laughter and chasing.

"I think," he announced a good while later, "we should eat now. C'mon, let's get dinner organised."

Jacob sat with Ashton on one side and Lily on the other as they watched a movie. His mind was drifting to Matisse. He wondered how she was going tonight. Whether she was coping or having a bad day.

He recalled the feeling of having her in his arms, like she was made for him ... and wishing he didn't have to let her go. He enjoyed her softness, and the sweet smell of coconut and frangipani he would always associate with her wherever he travelled in the South Pacific for business.

Lily was snuggled up against him, almost asleep. Jacob threw the remote control onto the coffee table. "Time for bed I think, Miss Lily." He carried the sleepy girl to her bedroom. By the time she went to the bathroom and climbed into bed she had roused herself enough for a story. She pointed to the one she wanted, and Jacob obliged, stretching out next to her as she grabbed her favourite, well-worn teddy and tucked it under her arm.

"There you go, princess," he told her a few minutes later, as he leaned out and put the book back on the shelf, kissing Lily on the top of her head. "Hey, you've got a lot of artwork on your wall since I was here last."

"Matisse helped me," the little girl said sleepily. "She's an artist."

"Mmm, I know."

Lily sighed. "I think she is very pretty."

"You know what Lily, so do I, but don't tell anyone I said so, okay?"

"Oh alright. Mummy said Matisse was going to get married but Jonathan her fee, fio–fee–on–say," she stumbled over the unfamiliar word, "crashed his scooter and died. He didn't have his helmet on. Matisse was riding on the scooter too and she got hurt and was in hospital for a long time. Sometimes she limps a bit from her sore leg. Mummy says her heart is still hurting because she misses Jonathan and that's why she gets sad sometimes."

"That's right."

"Mummy thinks you might be able to help fix her heart up so she's not so sad anymore."

"Oh, does she now? Well, I guess I'll see what I can do." Jacob got up, smoothed the unicorn doona cover and flicked off the light. "Goodnight, sleep tight, don't fall out of bed tonight," he told her, reciting the rhyme from his childhood night-time ritual.

"Right, Ash my man, game on," he told his nephew as he was handed a Playstation control.

LATER, once Ashton was in bed, Jacob fired up his laptop and got stuck into the work. He had to push all thoughts of Matisse out of his head, and that took some doing.

His coffee sat largely untouched as he worked his way through his to-do list: managers' weekly reports, signing off on press releases, casting an eye over the latest marketing campaign, requests for charitable donations.

The hard yards of the last fifteen years meant that Jacob could, if he so desired, take his foot off the accelerator and start to enjoy some of the spoils of his success, but he didn't see the need to live larger than life. He wasn't in need of a collection of sports cars. Of course, he appreciated a fine set of wheels, and he'd owned a few memorable vehicles in his time. But he preferred to keep a low profile, so driving a fancy car didn't fit in with that ideal. True, he had spent a considerable sum on the residence he now called home, but his accommodation prior to that had been very modest. Most of his money had been poured back into growing his business operations.

For the first time though, he had come to the realisation that the success he had worked so hard to achieve would be better served if he had someone to share it with. Which of course led him back to Matisse. Was she someone he wanted to share his success with, his life? He'd shied away from relationships in recent years. Was he ready to launch out and take a risk with Matisse? He'd like to—but was she prepared to take a risk with him? She'd been so hurt after Jonno's death ...

He sighed and turned his attention back to his job list, crossing another task off.

He lost track of time, and looked up in surprise when Adam and Melanie walked through the door. He glanced at the time displayed on the bottom right-hand corner of the laptop before he shut it down and closed the lid.

"How was your night?"

"Good thanks, Jacob," Mel replied.

"You know how much we appreciate you kid-sitting for us," Adam told him.

"Hey, I don't mind at all," he said, stretching after sitting for so long. They caught up for a while before Mel excused herself. Adam walked out to the car with him.

"So, when are you planning to make a move on Matisse?" Adam probed.

"Sorry?"

"C'mon man, I know you are more than interested."

Jacob sighed. "It's not that straightforward, Adam."

"Because why?"

"You know because why. One word: Jonno. At the moment, there doesn't seem to be any way around him. She's still back there somewhere with him, and can't seem to move on with her life."

"Whether you like it or not, Jonno is always going to be part of her life in some form. I can't imagine how tough it would've been then ... and probably now as well. You can't expect her to simply stop loving him."

"I know that." Jacob sighed. "And I wouldn't expect her to— I just hoped there would be room there for me as well ... but I don't know ..."

"You two would be so good together."

"So my sister keeps telling me. But until Matisse gives me a chance, we won't know for sure, will we?"

"Well, if it's any consolation, we know she's interested in you."

"Interested is one thing, a physical and emotional connection is another matter altogether."

"I'm pretty sure those are there as well. Mel and I can tell, every time your name comes up in conversation with her. Ash and Lily love her to bits already. Both Mel and I think highly of her. You couldn't go far wrong if you chose to pursue her."

"Like I said, it's not that simple. I'm trying to give her some space and time to maybe come around to the idea that I'd like to have a relationship with her that's a bit more than just friendship ..." he trailed off.

"Maybe you need a big gesture to sweep her off her feet or something."

Jacob was noncommittal.

"Just don't give up on her. She'll be worth it, you know that."

"Yeah, I know."

"We'll just have to keep reminding her how awesome you are."

Jacob grimaced.

"No, seriously. The kids already do that, anyway. It can't hurt to plant a few more seeds there."

"Just don't lay it on too thick."

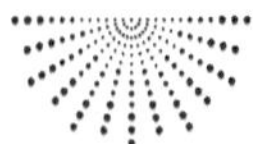

"Tomorrow is going to be a huge day," he warned her. "I'm picking you up before first light."

Matisse wrinkled her nose.

"Lucky for you, it's not daylight savings time yet. You'll need warm clothes, something to wear out for dinner later ... and don't forget your camera gear."

Matisse still wasn't sure why she had agreed to the day out with him. No, actually, that was a lie. Matisse enjoyed her time with Jacob, and the chance to do something away from the confines of the Cape was tempting. Jacob was becoming more irresistible the more she got to know him. Thoughtful, compassionate and hardworking. She admired the close relationship he had with his family. He adored his nieces and nephews, and they adored him. He seemed popular and respected in town and was a successful businessman. Oh, and he was easy on the eye.

Intrigued at what the day might hold, Matisse sat waiting for Jacob on the cabin steps, leaning up against the stair rail. She stifled a yawn as the Ranger pulled up in front of her.

JACOB HAD PUT a lot of thought into planning the day. It had taken a bit of convincing to get her to agree to go. By the end, he hoped ... well he just wanted to see what eventuated.

He opened the car door as she stood and stretched, then leaned back to grab her camera bag and another larger one he assumed contained clothes for later. Her jeans were complemented by cute but practical zip-up black ankle boots. A thick, dark green jacket was matched by a knitted beanie in the same colour. He stowed the gear she handed over, and pulled a travel mug of coffee out of one of the cup holders and gave it to her before starting the engine.

MATISSE WAS CONFUSED when they pulled up at his place a short time later. "Okay, what's going on?"

"We're flying out." He pulled her stuff out of the vehicle and walked over to the chopper.

"You're not serious?"

"Jump in."

She ducked, and pulled herself awkwardly into the helicopter. Jacob did the pre-flight checks as she settled in beside him, in awe of the bank of gauges, lights and switches on the flight control panel between them. She couldn't help but take a deep breath of his "just showered" scent as he reached around her, took the end of the seatbelt, and made sure it was securely fastened. He put a headset on her and adjusted it, so she was able to hear him.

He started the engine, lifted up out of the clearing, and skimmed the trees as he banked for the Lightstation. Apprehensive about going aloft, Matisse had to trust the pilot. It was too dark to enjoy the view, but Jacob promised to fly over on the return trip. She barely had time to take it all in before they were back on the ground at the joy-flight area of the Twelve Apostles.

"The best time to see this area is at dawn when there aren't so many tourists around." Jacob pulled on a backpack and handed Matisse her camera before striding off past the dimly lit visitors' centre towards the highway. Taking the left-hand path, the gravel crunched underfoot as she followed him down and under the road, across the access area to the top of the Gibson Steps, where he waited until she caught up to him.

"The steps are named after Hugh Gibson, who owned the Glenample Homestead near here. He was supposed to have carved them to be able to reach the beach. Some people believe they were originally made by the Kirrae Whurrong people. As you can see, they've since been concreted." Jacob's history lesson was a welcome distraction as they walked down the eighty-six steps. Counting every one, she leaned heavily on the metal handrail.

"You know the Loch Ard ship was wrecked not too far from here?" She nodded and he went on, "There were only two survivors. A cabin boy and a young female passenger. When they were found they were taken to Glenample to recover."

It was slow going for Matisse, but she was determined to make it down to the beach, positive the effort would be well worth her discomfort. Scanning the beach area in the pre-dawn light, she quickly found a vantage point and set up her tripod, screwing the connection into the baseplate of her camera and clipping it on to the top. The sheer scale of the cliff line and the ruggedness of the huge forty-five metre limestone stacks offshore were very humbling. Matisse had to remind herself to look up and enjoy the vista rather than just focus on the camera viewfinder. Scattered puffs of cloud glowed pink above the twin formations known as Gog and Magog. Closer to the horizon, the light had created a lilac haze. As the sun came up, the changing colours took her breath away. Jacob stood quietly near her as she clicked away. Quiet serenity with no one else about— a far cry from her previous experience.

Eventually, Matisse stretched, and remembered her companion. Looking behind her, she saw he had moved about twenty metres away and set up a picnic breakfast. He sat waiting for her to join him, handing her a steaming mug of coffee as soon as she reached the rug. Making use of the rock as a backrest, she stretched out to enjoy the scenery.

"Okay, I'm seriously impressed." She indicated the spread of fruit and pastries between them. "Breakfast and a stunning view —a lovely way to begin the day, I will admit."

~

"I'T'S ONLY THE START," he promised, feeding her some strawberries, keeping it light between them, holding back with great effort. *Be patient, don't push.*

Reluctantly, they eventually packed up. Jacob pulled Matisse to her feet. She winced a bit.

"Are you going to manage the stairs?" he asked.

"Not sure, to be honest. Going up will be much tougher."

"In that case, you wait here. I'll be back shortly." He hurried back to the top of the steps.

~

MATISSE LEANED BACK against the rock, drinking in the view. He was right, it was much better at this hour without the hordes of tourists clamouring for their photos. She closed her eyes. Breathe. Still. Calm. Repeat. It was so peaceful.

"What the …?" The quiet had been shattered by the sound of a helicopter coming over the cliff. Jacob manoeuvred the chopper down to where she waited. She shook her head in amazement as he landed on the beach.

Leaving the controls, he took her by the hand and led her back to the chopper. He handed her the headset and adjusted it and his own before pulling into the air and flying the helicopter as far as the Bay of Islands, then looping around Cape Otway itself and then on to Melbourne.

Matisse started to relax and enjoy the journey. "Awestruck" was a pretty good word to describe how she was feeling. She made a conscious decision to be in the moment and enjoy the scenery and not take photos, but she didn't realise how hard it would be to resist. She was familiar of course with this stretch of coastline. Like a lot of Australians, she had seen photos and promotional clips, but to actually be there overhead to witness the early morning light hitting the rock formations for herself was beyond anything she could have imagined.

Jacob heard her exclamations through his headset.

"Oh wow, I can't believe you get to do this on a regular basis. This view is incredible. Thanks for bringing me up here."

Jacob kept up a running commentary for her as he hugged the coastline and then buzzed Geelong on the way through. He was pleased Matisse was enthralled by the whole experience. Once they hit Melbourne, Jacob did a fifteen-minute circuit, taking in the Westgate Bridge and its surrounds. The large red and white *Spirit of Tasmania* ferry was docked at the port. They flew via Albert Park as Jacob pointed out the street circuit of the Grand Prix, then, the iconic roller-coaster and laughing-mouth entrance of St Kilda's Luna Park. Flying over the beachside bathing boxes at Brighton, Matisse was shocked to learn that the lease on one of the small brightly coloured timber buildings without power or water had gone for over three hundred thousand dollars. They counted backyard tennis courts in the leafy, affluent suburb of Toorak. The South Eastern Freeway followed the Yarra River and they did the same, checking out the Royal Botanic Gardens and the white majesty of Government House and other landmarks such as the Rod Laver Arena and Melbourne Cricket Ground—or "The G" as it was affectionately known—the scene for many an epic cricket match or AFL game.

Jacob flew north out of the city and up to the Yarra Valley, coming in to land in a grassy field near a distinctive, low, brown building. He killed the engine, pulled off his headset, and walked around to the other side of the helicopter where he took her hand as she alighted.

"THIS WAY TO LUNCH," he told her over the din of the slowing rotor. She walked with him towards the building which she discovered was a chocolatier. They joined a tour of the premises and sampled some of the treats on offer. By the time they reached the cafe for lunch, Matisse wasn't all that hungry. The company was engaging though. They swapped stories about growing up and school days. Matisse felt herself being drawn to him the longer they spent together.

"You about ready to get back in the air?" he asked, pushing back from the table.

"Sure," she told him, grasping his hand as he escorted her back to the waiting helicopter. Their departure caused a bit of a stir amongst the other visitors.

THE FLIGHT back to the Cape was equally enthralling to Matisse, and she was sorry when he finally brought the helicopter in to land next to his house. "I can see why you love flying so much, Jacob."

"I'm glad you enjoyed yourself. I'll let you into the house if you'd like to go and freshen up. Then we'll get going again."

"Where to this time?"

"You'll have to wait and see, but I think you will enjoy the change of pace." A short time later she climbed into the Ranger and before long they were driving through a heavily timbered area with majestic blue gums and mountain ash. It was late afternoon before they reached the next destination. Matisse could catch a glimpse of water between the trees.

"Have you heard of Lake Elizabeth?"

"Isn't that where they have the platypus ecotours?"

"That's right. Well, Lake Elizabeth isn't the only place around here with platypus." Jacob pulled up alongside another four-wheel drive. The sandy-haired driver came over to Jacob's window. "Hey Tony, how's it going?"

"Jacob, good to see you again."

"This is Matisse. I was hoping you might be able to show her a platypus or two."

"Can't make any promises, but we'll give it a go." Matisse tagged along behind the two men with her camera gear as they walked down a "work in progress" wooden boardwalk to a small landing beside the mirror-calm surface of the lake. There were already three life jackets hanging on pegs on the rail at the end of the boardwalk. Tony, she learned, was the caretaker tasked with overseeing the development of hiking trails and the establishment of a number of cabins to one day allow visitors to stay on the property.

"Lake Elizabeth was formed after a landslip in heavy rain about fifty years ago on the Barwon River. This, however, is a result of a clumsy effort to divert a river." Tony helped Matisse into the olive-green canoe. Jacob handed her the camera bag.

"Lucky for you, Tony and I will do the paddling. You can concentrate on taking photos."

While Jacob stepped into the rear position, Tony untied the canoe, pushed it away from its mooring, and climbed in with practised ease. The two men quickly got into sync and set off across the water.

Matisse had seen photos of Lake Elizabeth, and to her mind this was equally spectacular. Green framed the lake edges. Ghostly white trees with their tops missing stood sentinel along the far side, reflected in the water. Behind them the blackwoods' majestic height raised a salute to the afternoon light. The beauty of the place took her breath away as she tried to capture the scenery around her, easily imagining how magical it would be with early morning mist spreading its tendrils across the expanse of water. Another Otway jewel.

The canoe hardly made a sound as they made their way to the far side. Neither did the various ducks gliding serenely along to the right of them. The same couldn't be said of the black cockatoos, their piercing screeches shattering the quiet. Jacob pointed out superb wrens as they flitted in and out of the undergrowth on the bank. Yellow robins played chase through the greenery.

The paddlers grounded the canoe, putting some cattle egrets to flight from the shallows in the process, and helped Matisse climb out. The trio sat quietly on the foreshore and waited.

Birdlife continued to show off around them. Yellow honeyeaters pinged the nearby heathland as they searched for their next snack. Reed warblers perched amongst the bulrushes, their chirping joining the avian choir.

Jacob eventually tapped Matisse on the arm and pointed. A platypus had come to the water's edge about five metres from where they were sitting. The slick grey fur ball, with its duckbill and beaver-like tail, scrabbled around feeding for a good ten minutes before disappearing.

Jacob looked over at Matisse and locked eyes with her. She was glowing. He reached over and patted her leg. She put her hand on top of his, whispering her thanks. If Tony hadn't been right there next to them, he might have been tempted to reach over and kiss her there and then. It was an incredible moment, but the day wasn't over yet.

AFTER A QUICK CUPPA with Tony back at his nearby cabin, Matisse and Jacob both changed their clothes for dinner. There was more driving. Jacob promised it would be worth the effort and he hadn't been wrong so far, so Matisse just had to trust him. She had to admit though, by the time they drove through the white timber farm gates of the country restaurant, she was well and truly ready to eat. There were casement windows all along the side of the renovated farmhouse and it was lit up both inside and out. Elegant, warm and inviting.

Jacob held the car door open for her. She'd opted for black linen trousers and a matching jacket, over a white short-sleeved blouse with a lace collar, adding a splash of red with her necklace. She hadn't thought she would need any dressy outfits, but thankfully she'd thrown this one in at the last minute after Dee insisted: "Just in case you decide to go out somewhere. You never know."

Jacob also wore black trousers and a white shirt, no tie, top button undone and a black leather jacket. The staff all seemed to recognise Jacob, greeting him by name.

"Do you come here often?"

"On the odd occasion, but lately I've been too busy."

They walked past the round, white-clothed tables to where they would be sitting. Jacob pulled out a grey chair and waited for her to settle in.

As Matisse took in the ambience in the soft lighting, she felt Jacob studying her features. He held her gaze when she turned back to him. Matisse ducked her head, pretending to study the night's menu, not able to look at him any longer. His dark eyes were almost melting her where she sat. Her stomach swirled as she hitched a breath. Her heart rate picked up, her face warm under his penetrating gaze.

She was having trouble concentrating. "I ... um ... can't decide what to have?"

"You actually don't have to choose, Matisse. We get to eat everything."

"What do you mean ... everything?"

"Exactly that—tonight's dinner is literally everything listed there in front of you."

"Oh ... really?" He nodded. She cast her eye over the menu. There had to be a dozen or more dishes listed. That would take them a while to get through. Hours maybe. Matisse took in what she hoped was a subtle deep breath. How was she ever going to last that length of time if Jacob was going to keep up the intensity of his gaze?

"We can choose to have wine paired with the food, but as I'm driving, I'm opting for the non-alcoholic beverages."

"That's fine by me as well."

There was a procession of tasty morsels. Food so different to anything she had eaten before. Who would have thought that green ants tasted like citrus?

Surprisingly, after the first couple of dishes were out of the way, she started to relax as their conversation flowed as easily as it had at lunchtime. Naturally, the food was discussed in some detail as it arrived, with Jacob adding insights to the server's comments.

"Wait till you taste this," Jacob told her as their waiter set another plate before them. "I remember reading a review some-where that compared eating oyster ice cream to ducking into a brisk ocean wave."

"Goodness. I can see what they meant," she agreed, after sampling the dish. Then there was the smoked eel doughnut—long fingers of fried pastry, reminiscent of Spanish churros.

Her tastebuds were on overload. Actually, every one of her senses was on overload as course after delectable course arrived at the table. And the bread? Totally sigh-inducing!

A tall slim man with short brown hair and dressed in chef's whites came over and shook hands with Jacob.

"I was told you were dining with us tonight, but I didn't hear the chopper. It's been a while, Jacob."

"It has. Actually, I was in the air most of the day. We flew to Melbourne and out to the Yarra for lunch."

"The Chocolatier?"

"Yes ... and we've just come from the lake."

"Did you see any platypus?"

"As matter of fact, we did."

"You've packed a lot into the day."

"And it's not over yet. Dan, I'd like you to meet Matisse. Dan is the owner and head chef."

"Pleased to meet you, Matisse. I hope you are enjoying your dining experience with us this evening."

"Yes, very much," Matisse answered. "I don't have enough words in my vocabulary to do justice to the food."

"Dan has ... what? ... about thirty acres here? And they grow most of their own food or source produce from nearby farms. The menu is totally dependent on what is available on the day." He looked at Dan. "I believe congratulations are in order. Another award last month. Well done."

"Thanks, it's great to be recognised for all the hard work the staff put in. I have a wonderful team here," he told Matisse. After chatting for a few more minutes, he left to check on the other diners.

Matisse and Jacob quickly fell into conversation about their day in general. There were so many ideas from the day that were competing for attention in her head, she knew she was going to be flat out over the next few weeks getting her visions onto canvas. But she was excited by the prospect and couldn't wait to get started. Thank goodness another shipment of canvas was due to arrive next week.

Jacob asked a couple of insightful questions that started her talking about her artwork, and he seemed genuinely interested in the processes she used while painting. It would be oh-too-easy to talk the rest of the night away about her art—her passion.

The grand finale to the meal was the signature parsnip cone

that shattered to reveal an apple and parsnip mousse. Sublimely satisfying.

Matisse finally pulled the serviette off her lap and tossed it on the table in front of her, a little disappointed their time here was at an end. "That was the best meal I've ever eaten."

"Good to hear." Jacob smiled, placing his credit card in the black folder sitting next to him on the table. He leaned forward in his chair. "I have one last surprise for you."

Matisse raised her eyebrows at him. "I really don't think you can possibly top this, Jacob."

He signed off on the bill and came around to pull her seat out. "Actually, I think I can."

"How much further?" They seemed to have been driving for a very long time.

"Almost there, but you will have to walk a bit, so you might want to change your shoes and grab your warmer jacket. The camera gear comes as well."

"Why's that?"

"You'll see."

He eventually stopped, seemingly in the middle of nowhere, and led the way up along a narrow track to the top of a hill. They walked in silence; Matisse had her head down, concentrating on the darkened trail in front of her.

Jacob knew there was no guarantee that the lights would even show tonight. He'd been keeping a close watch on the news reports and there had been some visibility over the last couple of days, so he was hoping tonight would be the same.

He. Was. In. Luck.

The lightshow from the Aurora Australis was a sight to

behold. There were only a handful of places on the Victorian mainland where you could catch a glimpse of the southern lights, and this was one. Which was the main reason he'd purchased the property in the first place; he had plans to eventually develop an ecolodge on site. The southern lights were a rarity but totally stunning.

Matisse seemed utterly speechless and stood transfixed by the spectacle of the night sky. The dark purples gave way to pinks and yellows with blues mixed in as well. The multitude of stars dotted the sky like sequins on a beautiful evening dress.

"You might like to take some photos," Jacob prompted her.

"What? ... Oh, yes, of course." He helped her put up the tripod, and she set the camera to a long exposure and stood silently soaking it all in. It lasted maybe forty minutes and then the sky faded. The moon and stars took centre stage once again. Matisse started to pack up her gear. "How did you know about this spot?"

"Oh ... I know the owner quite well."

"You were absolutely right," she told him, zipping up her camera bag. "You totally topped the day." She turned and looked him in the eyes without wavering. "Thank you so much, Jacob. I've had the most beautiful, magical day."

In that moment, he knew it was time.

"Matisse," he said softly. "I'd like to kiss you—is that okay?" Her nod was barely perceptible. "Are you sure?"

She closed her eyes briefly, then opened them and nodded, holding his gaze in the moonlight. Jacob pulled her slowly in against him. He liked how she fitted in his arms, and the sweet smell of her was intoxicating.

His hand went to the side of her face, gently caressing her cheek with the back of his fingers as he leaned in. He had been waiting so long for her to be willing, and he had no idea if he'd ever get the opportunity again, so he was just going to savour every bit of her.

There was a brief gentle kiss and then another slightly longer one. He felt her hands against his chest. Jake knew he should stop, but he just wanted a little more. As he deepened the kiss, her hands moved behind his head. He was going to pull back, but she held him there and returned his kiss with one of her own. That, was worth the wait. He enjoyed her, perhaps too much. Pausing, he looked down at her in his arms and held her against his chest. Her arms went around his waist and she stood there for a long time.

He kissed the top of her head and rested his cheek there, inhaling the scent of her. She had made a huge step towards him and he was overwhelmed by how strong his feelings were in that moment. It wasn't going to be an easy journey for her. He also knew that she still needed space and time and, above all, understanding, but he was sure she was on her way to him.

He bent to retrieve her camera gear and slung the bag over his shoulder. As he tucked the tripod under one arm, his free hand caught hers, lacing their fingers together. She seemed content to walk back to the Ranger hand in hand. Jacob stowed her gear in the back of the ute and opened the door. She paused before she got in, and he just had to kiss her again. She willingly went into his arms, running her fingers through his hair as he threaded his fingers through her long tresses. There was a lot more fervour this time as she pressed in closer. Later, he couldn't understand how he had managed to restrain himself, but he didn't want to scare her off.

He drove with one hand on the steering wheel while he reached over to take her hand and kiss her fingers. She was quiet. Very quiet. When he had to let go of her fingers to change gears, she rested her hand lightly on his thigh and he covered her hand with the warmth of his own.

～

Matisse wriggled around trying to find a comfortable position in Jake's car, struggling to stay awake at the very late hour.

Allowing Jake to kiss her was finally giving herself permission to admit she had strong feelings towards him. Matisse knew he had strong feelings as well. He had been very patient as she tried to find a way forward.

That second kiss had awakened something in her that she thought had died along with Jonno. It was intense, and caught her by surprise.

By the time he pulled up outside the cabin, she realised she wanted to spend the night with him—but going the next step was a commitment she was afraid to make.

JAKE SENSED SHE WAS WAVERING, but wanted her to be absolutely sure and not have any regrets. He wasn't about to push her, as much as he wanted to take her to bed. Releasing his seatbelt, he leaned over to kiss her. Matisse put her hand along his jaw and tenderly brushed her thumb across his lips. It was almost his undoing. He accepted and returned her kisses, but kept himself in the driver's seat as she lingered before finally getting out and pulling her belongings out of the car.

She didn't look back. He waited until she'd closed the door behind her, and he could see the glow of the lamp, then put the car into gear and reluctantly drove home.

CHAPTER FOURTEEN

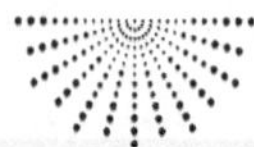

From the time Jacob had picked her up until well after she woke the next day, Matisse had hardly given Jonathan any thought. She recognised it as a huge break-through, if only short-lived. Matisse realised she was actually capable of having a good time without it being sabotaged by thoughts of her late fiancé. Maybe Jacob was right about her being able to enjoy another relationship.

But now, Matisse was puzzled. She thought her relationship with Jacob had moved to another level but, obviously, she was mistaken. Since what she had loosely termed their "big day out", Jacob had well and truly kept his distance, as if the shoe was now firmly on the other foot.

She waited to see who would be coming with him today. He'd chosen repair jobs that apparently couldn't be done on his own. It was either his father or Sam or both. One day, to her surprise, he had even brought Todd with him. He was careful never to be alone with her.

Today it was Sam. Again. The two men greeted her briefly before getting down to work, while she worked at her easel down by the creek. Matisse kept watch for a chance to get Jacob by himself.

Eventually, the opportunity presented itself. Sam had to make a mobile phone call and had driven off to find a few bars of reception. Jacob was measuring some timber. She dropped the paintbrush and walked over to him. He had his back to her, so he didn't see her approaching. As she moved round to stand in front of him, he barely glanced up and kept working.

"So, what's going on, Jacob?" she quizzed him. He refused to make eye contact. "Did I do or say something?"

"No."

"Sorry, I don't believe you. There must be something. You've hardly spoken to me since ... well ... for days, let alone let me get close to you." There was no response. Jacob just kept on working.

Finally, he answered, "Basically, you are messing with my head." He used her own line back at her. "I'm strongly attracted to you and having trouble keeping you at arm's length. Because I want more than I think you're ready for, I've decided a hands-off policy would be safer ... for both of us ..."

Matisse kept moving to try and get him to look at her, but he was just as determined not to. She thought she was ready for more, but now she was confused and had no idea how to respond. Maybe arm's length was a good idea, but if she was honest, that's not where she wanted to be.

He heard her exasperation as she turned and went back to her easel. It was only then Jacob permitted himself to glance up at her retreating figure. What he really wanted to do was go after her, and take her in his arms and kiss any thoughts of Jonno out of her head.

He sighed as he reminded himself it had to be her choice to come to him, without reservation and without Jonno holding her back. Matisse was struggling, he could tell, with what he'd said. Maybe there were some tears there, but she needed to sort herself out without him clouding her judgement by being too close. It was killing him to do it, though.

A clatter attracted his attention. The easel was on the ground. She stood there, arms crossed, looking at him. Her loose hair was held back by a brightly coloured bandanna. The striped baggy pants and loose, flowing caramel top she was wearing reminded him of a 60s flower child. A very annoyed one at that.

He put his head down and kept working, praying that she wouldn't storm over to him, otherwise he wouldn't be able to keep his distance. Out of the corner of his eye he saw her march off along the creek. Once she was out of sight, he walked across to right the easel, putting the canvas back on the stand, then went on working, grateful that Sam had returned.

But his brother-in-law had a piece of him. "What is going on with you two?" he asked.

Jacob just shrugged.

"Whatever it is can you sort it out? Because the two of you are driving me crazy."

"MATISSE, would you come out on the lunch run with me tomorrow?" Mel asked Matisse late one afternoon after she had checked in.

"Sorry, what's that?"

"My turn to take Jake and his walkers their lunch." Matisse knew he was out leading one of the walks along the Great Ocean Road. "I get it ready first thing, drive out to the meeting point, and set it all up so that when they arrive it's all ready to go. Then clean up afterwards and come home. Jake usually asks the family to cater the lunches when he's leading. So, it's my turn. I could do with a hand. Lexie usually helps me, but she's away this week. Jacob suggested you might be willing to help."

Matisse wasn't so sure it was a good idea, but her friend needed the extra pair of hands she could provide, even if it meant seeing Jacob again. "Sure, I guess so. What time do we need to start?"

"Will around seven-thirty be okay? We'll need the time to prep and pack it up. It takes about an hour and a half to drive there and then we need to set up everything."

"Okay, but you will have to come and get me if I sleep in." Although Matisse knew that was unlikely, as she was in the habit of getting up early to make as much use of the daylight hours as possible to paint.

"Righto, are you coming in for dinner?" Matisse nodded. "I'll send one of the kids to get you when it's ready."

Matisse always enjoyed her time with Adam, Mel and their two. She certainly felt at home, and as a bonus got to hear stories of Jacob and his siblings growing up.

MATISSE HAD her hair pulled back into a ponytail when she arrived, wearing jeans and the navy embroidered polo shirt Mel had given her the night before. Melanie, likewise dressed, had taped a piece of paper to the bench listing the food required and its preparation.

The two women steadily worked their way down the list, Matisse doing whatever Mel asked. The cold meats and salads were packed into containers, then into eskies with ice. Drinks went into another. Adam was on hand to help load the four-wheel drive with the tables, chairs, plates and cups, cutlery, tablecloths. There was a mixed case of fruit and containers of homemade slice and biscuits. A couple of thermoses of hot water were also packed. Adam had designed and built a removable storage system for the back of their car which they used for their own camping trips, but it did double duty for days like today. Matisse watched as Adam and Mel packed the gear with practised ease. Everything had its place.

"Thanks, hon." Mel kissed Adam as he shut the tailgate. "See you later."

"Drive safely, okay?"

"Like I'm going to drive like a maniac all of a sudden," she teased, and kissed him again. Sighing inwardly as Adam waved them off, Matisse once again envied their close relationship. Surprisingly, she didn't find herself missing her former fiancé. Once, not so long ago, he would have been in her immediate thoughts, but now he was being relegated to part of her life that seemed so long ago. Whether he belonged there or not remained to be seen.

Mel pulled out of the motel driveway and headed in the direction of Warrnambool, not that they would be driving quite that far. Once they were out on the road, Matisse quizzed her about the walking tours.

"Jacob started doing these tours about eleven, no, twelve years ago. He gradually built it up from scratch, to where it is now. Initially there was one walk every six weeks. Nowadays tours leave every three or four days in the peak season. Off-peak it's about every seven to ten. Originally, they camped, but most of the places were shut down for conservation and land rehabilitation. So, then he had to find suitable accommodation. Man, some of the places were so old and daggy when he first got them. It was all hands on deck to get them habitable. Eventually, he built the business up enough to knock them down and start over. Real, boutique, eco-friendly lodges. The helicopters came about eight years ago—it seemed a natural progression. Jake loves flying."

"So I gathered."

"Most of his clients are high-end. Sometimes he picks them up from the airport and flies them out and around the Lightstation and the Apostles and so on, then they do the five-day walk and he flies them back to Melbourne."

"Sounds impressive."

"Oh, and he runs similar operations out of Broome in the north of Western Australia, and also across in Tasmania."

"Keeps him busy then?"

"Yeah, he's worked incredibly hard to get where he is today. He's been totally focused on building the business, probably to the detriment of his personal life ... Oh, he's had a couple of relationships over the years, the last probably four years ago. Since then, he's had no time, or should I say, he's not made any time, to pursue a relationship."

Melanie kept her eyes on the road as she talked. "I'm not sure if there is anything going on between you two, but whatever it is, he's been a lot more relaxed lately. It's good to see him slowing down a bit, instead of flying off around the place all the time ... my folks have noticed it as well, so they're pleased. They think you are having a good influence on him."

Matisse had her eyes fixed out the side window while Mel spoke.

"Is there anything going on between the two of you?"

Gee I don't know—I thought there was but now I'm not sure anymore—I'm so confused at the moment. I think I'm falling for your brother, but I don't know if he feels the same way.

"I ... umm, maybe, I guess. I thought there was but now I'm not so sure. I like your brother and that ... but ... it's still early days yet. I'm still having trouble moving on from the accident, and it doesn't seem fair to Jacob to embark on a relationship while I'm not in a good headspace."

"What does Jacob think?"

"I know he's finding the whole Jonno thing hard to deal with, but it is what it is, at the moment. He seems prepared to wait around, which I find extraordinary."

"He obviously thinks you're worth it."

"Hardly. Maybe I'm just a convenient distraction."

"Oh, I think you're more than a convenient distraction. Speaking of distractions ..."

Mel flicked on the radio and it wasn't long before they were both singing along to the tunes of the day.

At the designated meeting point, Mel backed the four-wheel drive into position. First, they had to get the navy pop-up gazebos into place, which, thankfully, was relatively easy with Mel's expertise. They tied them down, then set out the fold-out tables, covered them with the navy tablecloths, and added enviro-friendly picnicware to the top. Mel tossed the camping chairs out of the car and Matisse tipped them out of their covers and set them around nearby.

Soon all they had to do was sit and wait. Mel took a call from Jacob.

"Okay. Yes, she's here. See you soon." She looked over at Matisse. "They are about ten minutes away, so we can start putting out the food. He said something about asking you for a big favour, but I've no idea what it's about."

JACOB WAS glad that Mel had managed to get Matisse to come along and help. He was keen to see her again, even if just for a short time. This tour had been particularly uncomfortable. It wasn't that he was unused to female attention. That was par for the course. Usually there was a bit of harmless flirting, with the women firmly at arm's length. If they weren't after his phone number for themselves, it was for a daughter, niece, neighbour or friend. Failing that, he would end up with several slips of paper handed to him on the sly, which he tossed in the bin as soon as he got home. A couple of times he was tempted to follow up, but he never did.

The group of ladies on this trip, however, he could only describe as predatory. They were trying his patience. The constant double entendres were wearing him down, and he had to continually bite his tongue in an effort to continue to be charming and affable. And he still had two whole days to go!

Lord knows, he couldn't afford any negative publicity if he snapped.

Jacob hoped that Matisse would be willing to help him out, to try to stem the unwanted attention he was receiving.

MEL PUT her hands on her hips a short time later and looked at the setup, mentally checking off the list. "Hey Matisse, can you look for the serviettes? They should be in the third drawer on the right in the back of the car."

"Sure thing." Matisse was returning with the packet when the walkers started to arrive. She counted nine, plus Jacob. There was a group of five middle-aged women and two couples by the look of it. Jacob was wearing khaki knee-length hiking shorts and the same navy polo she and Mel were wearing. He also had a matching cap and a red bandanna around his neck. His sunglasses were hanging off the back of his neck as he relieved some of the walkers of their daypacks. He then pulled off his own much larger backpack and dumped it next to the others.

"Don't forget, I suggest taking your hiking boots off to give your feet a bit of a break if you are still not used to them. Looks like lunch is ready when you are, so help yourself."

He took his cap off and ran his fingers through his hair a couple of times, rescued his sunglasses and put them inside his upturned cap and left it on top of his backpack. He came over to the two girls who were standing off to the side. Matisse thought he looked a little on edge—maybe because of the favour he wanted. Even so, he looked mighty fine in his hiking clothes.

"Hey Mel, Matisse, thanks for coming."

She got straight to the point. "Your sister said you had a favour to ask."

"Yeah," he looked around to make sure the others were out of earshot. "I know this is going to sound a little crazy but ... I need you to pretend to be my girlfriend."

"O-kay," she drew the word out, hesitating. "Would you mind telling me why?"

"The ladies have been trying to hit on me ever since we started."

Mel snorted. "That's nothing new. I'm pretty sure you get hit on anytime there are women on the walks you lead."

"Ha, ha. They even managed to make sure I ended up in the water."

"So?" Mel raised an eyebrow at him.

"So, I couldn't win; either it was the wet shirt look or stripping off for a dry one."

Matisse remembered the day she found him shirtless by the creek—no wonder the ladies wanted to get him soaked.

Mel laughed. "They obviously like a bit of eye candy then."

Jacob took a swipe at his sister, but she just sidestepped him as the group of walkers started to mill around the food.

"The fearsome five are celebrating life after divorce. See the one in the low-cut pink top," he indicated, moving his head.

"Yeah." Matisse glanced at the forty-something bottle-blonde woman, who was wearing the minutest hiking shorts she had ever seen.

"That's the former Mrs West. She's the one who just finalised her divorce, and she thinks I'm fair game." Both girls were amused at his obvious discomfort.

"You're a big boy, I'm sure you can handle it—like you have every other time."

"Humpff, well about mid-afternoon yesterday, I cracked and told her I had a serious girlfriend."

"Don't suppose that had any effect?"

"No, you're right, but I thought if I produced 'said girlfriend' she might back off a bit."

Mel looked at Matisse. "Sounds a bit far-fetched to me, a bit too convenient for my liking. What do you think, Matisse?"

Matisse made the mistake of looking up at Jacob. As soon as

she caught the pleading look in his eyes, she knew she wouldn't be able to refuse his request.

Still it wouldn't hurt to keep him hanging for a few moments.

Matisse gave Mel a slow grin. "I'm willing to give him the benefit of the doubt."

"Thanks so much, Matisse." He took hold of her arm to lead her over to the group.

Mel warned him, "You know this could well come back to bite you somewhere down the track."

Jacob ignored his sister and kept walking.

"LADIES, I'd like you to meet Matisse, the girlfriend I was telling you about." His arm went to her shoulder and pulled her in against him for a side hug. There was an undercurrent in the group, that's for sure.

"So, you really do have a girlfriend, Jacob?" low-cut shirt said. "I thought you were making her up."

He planted a kiss on Matisse's cheek. He owed her big time.

"No, she's real enough, hey babe?"

Babe? Oh, really? Matisse was sure she could hear Mel chuckling in the background.

"Nice to meet you." Her gaze swept around the group.

"So how long have you two been an item?" one of the group asked.

"Oh, not long really. We only met a couple of months back."

"Jake told us you're an artist."

Matisse nodded. "Landscape mostly. I came down here for a change of scenery, which you will admit is pretty spectacular. It's not hard to find inspiration."

Low-cut shirt looked straight at Jacob. "The scenery is pretty spectacular. Haven't talked Jake into posing au naturel by any chance?"

Matisse was shocked at low-cut's audacity. "Umm, no, not yet."

"Well, when you do, honey, let me know and I'll be the first in line to buy the painting."

Good grief. No wonder Jacob wanted help.

She had no idea how to respond. "I'll keep that in mind. I had better go and help, so I will see you later." She pulled out of his grasp and walked back to Melanie, rolling her eyes as she reached her friend.

Jacob got a plate of food for himself and beckoned her to come and sit next to him.

"You go," Mel told her, shaking her head.

Jacob was a very attentive and affectionate boyfriend. Just for show of course, but Matisse was happy to take any scraps of affection he was willing to throw her way.

She was grateful for the reprieve from the distance he had been putting between them lately, and lapped it up greedily. The contingent of walkers for the most part accepted her presence with the group—except low-cut, but there were no surprises there, brazenly flirting with Jacob in front of Matisse. The harder low-cut went, the stronger Jacob's show of affection was towards Matisse, but it didn't seem to faze the older woman.

A couple of her friends tried not so subtly to rein her in.

Eventually the group started to reassemble. Jacob, along with the other two men, helped to fold the tables and slide them into the four-wheel drive, then took down the shade tents. The others folded their chairs and put them back into the bags, then stacked them next to the car. Jacob deliberately steered Matisse through the group and off to the side, out of earshot but still in the group's line of sight. He turned her and slid his palms down her arms. She shivered involuntarily as he took her hands. He brushed an errant wisp of hair back into place and ran his finger along the side of her face. She closed her eyes and took a deep breath.

"I'm so grateful you agreed to do this." Matisse looked up

and her gaze locked on his gorgeous brown eyes. She willed herself not to melt.

~

"I'M GOING to kiss you now," he warned. He'd been wanting a repeat performance ever since their day together but was worried he wouldn't be able to stop.

"What about your hands-off policy?" she asked.

"Desperate times call for desperate measures," he joked, "and besides there is an audience, so I won't be able to get carried away."

~

WELL MAYBE IT won't stop me. Before he could pull her in for a kiss, she seized the initiative, reached up and pulled his face down, planting a smouldering kiss on his unsuspecting lips. She pulled back slightly. *Whew.*

"Will that do?" she asked innocently, taking in his slightly dazed features.

"Um yeah, I think so."

"There's plenty more where that came from," she challenged. His response was immediate. Matisse grabbed onto the front of his polo shirt to steady herself as his mouth covered hers. Everything else faded away as she lost herself in his kiss that was over way too soon for her liking. He pulled her in for a hug and stroked her hair.

"I'd better be going," he murmured, his voice husky as he let her go.

"Hope it helps," she told him. Matisse stood watching as he went over to retrieve his sunglasses, shoving his cap back on his head. She couldn't help but admire his backside in the fitted shorts as he hoisted his backpack. Reluctantly she turned to leave, glancing back to give him a half wave before sticking her hands in her pockets and walking back to Melanie. She had to stop herself from running after him for one more kiss.

Mel raised an eyebrow at her friend. "That was quite convincing."

"Thank you, I think."

~

Wow.

Here he was worrying he was the one who would get carried away.

Matisse certainly surprised him.

Damn, if he didn't want to turn right around and go back for more.

He couldn't wipe the grin off his face as he joined the group. One of the guys whistled as his wife fanned herself with her hat. He accepted their teasing with good humour.

Maybe the rest of the walk would be less stressful and if not, the high from the kiss he'd shared with Matisse would sustain him. Making his way to the front of the walkers, they fell into line behind him.

He glanced back. Matisse and Mel were watching them leave. He gave a wave and continued walking with added spring in his step.

CHAPTER FIFTEEN

The kitchen at Pembroke was crowded when Jacob walked in with Matisse, one evening a few nights later.

His mother and Andrea were busy with the finishing touches for dinner. Sam was on dish duty with Ben. Mel and Adam were getting all lovey-dovey at the well-worn timber table where Jacob's father sat at the end, engrossed in the newspaper. Ashton and Luke were in the process of taking cutlery to the dining room while Lily and her cousin Molly were drawing alongside their grandfather.

Jacob slipped the large parcel he was carrying out of harm's way as Mel caught his eye. She shot him a grin, acknowledging the shift in the dynamics of the relationship between him and Matisse. Mel seemed pleased they were on their way to becoming a couple. He knew bringing Matisse along to a family dinner spoke volumes.

Matisse was sporting a country look tonight rather than the loose, flowing boho look she favoured. She blended right in with the women of his family, wearing jeans and a fitted, pale pink three-quarter-sleeve blouse. Her hair was loose and flowing for a change—just how he liked it.

"Evening all." There was a chorus of, "Hi Uncle Jake," from the younger family members.

"What are you doing here?" Adam joked at Matisse. "Have you come to run the gauntlet of a Davis family dinner?"

"Apparently."

"You really don't want to do this," Sam continued.

"I'd be going while you still have a chance," Adam added.

Matisse decided to play along and attempted to make a break for it. Jacob caught her around the waist. "Not so fast, Sunshine."

"Oh, now you're done for." That was Adam. Matisse pretended to struggle. Jake just put his arms around her and swung her feet off the ground. A commotion ensued as Sam and Adam both lunged for Jake at the same time. They grappled him so Matisse could free herself. There was a lot of shrieking from the kids.

"Run, Matisse."

"Don't look back!"

She stopped on the other side of the kitchen table. Adam and Sam each held one of Jake's arms behind his back. Matisse regarded them with some amusement as Jake shrugged his shoulders apologetically.

"Thanks, boys," she said. "I appreciate your concern, but if it's all the same with you, I'll take my chances."

"You can't be serious?"

"Poor girl, you must be delirious."

"Quite possibly," she admitted.

"Okay, don't say you weren't warned." They made a big show of lifting their hands up to release Jake.

"Gentlemen." He nodded to his brothers-in-law and straightened his navy button-down shirt.

Matisse slid into the seat next to Mel. "Is it always this crazy?"

"Pretty much."

"What have I gotten myself into?" she asked with a smile at

Jake. Putting his hands up, he shook his head then went around to greet his mother, who had been ignoring the nonsense. He swiped a piece of roast potato and got his hand slapped for his trouble.

"Fine example you're setting for your children," was James Davis's only comment to his sons-in-law, without looking up from the paper.

"Couldn't agree more, Dad," Jake told him, coming over to pat him on the shoulder to the sound of Adam's disgusted snort in the background.

"Did we miss anything?" Todd asked as he arrived with a gorgeous petite brunette by his side. They were both wearing jeans with white t-shirts. Todd topped his with an unbuttoned long-sleeve red plaid shirt rolled up to the elbows. The girl wore a short black jacket and her long hair was twisted into a messy bun. She looked effortlessly chic with minimal makeup.

Adam spoke first. "We were just warning Matisse about the perils of a Davis family dinner. Are you sure it's wise to bring her here?"

"Guys, this is Sylvie, from France, currently backpacking her way around the country." Todd introduced her to everyone. Sylvie didn't seem at all fazed. Matisse waited to be introduced.

"Bonsoir, Sylvie," she told the other girl. Sylvie's dark blue eyes lit up.

"Ah, so you speak French?"

Matisse paused briefly. "A little. I'm out of practice though. How are you coping with my friend there?"

"He's okay."

Matisse had to think how to translate her next comments. She said, in French, "Be warned, he has a reputation as a ladies' man."

"Yes, I already worked that out."

"You are very brave then."

The French girl nodded at her.

"What was that all about?" Todd demanded.

"Just giving her a 'heads up' about you, that's all."

"Great."

"But it seems your reputation has preceded you." She winked at Sylvie and continued in French, "It might be fun to mess with him a little."

"Oui."

Jake leaned down to her.

"You keeping up?" she asked him quietly, in English.

"Enough to get the general idea."

She reverted to French. "It's about time your brother got some payback," she told him, or words to that effect.

EVERYONE MADE their way into the dining room. The large table accommodated the ten adults with ease. There was a simple rustic timber and flower arrangement in the centre, and natural woven placemats instead of a tablecloth. Tall glasses with a delicate engraved floral design graced each setting. A smaller table had been added to the end for the five grandchildren to use. A mini floral arrangement sat there along with green plastic drink cups for each child.

James Davis presided over the gathering from his place at the end of the table. Claire sat on his right with Andrea, Sam, Adam and Melanie, who supervised the youngsters. Jacob sat opposite his mother alongside Matisse who made sure Sylvie sat next to her with Todd. James got everyone's attention and acknowledged Matisse and Sylvie for coming before giving thanks for the food. He carved the massive roast in front of him, and started loading the plates as they were passed to him.

The rest of the family helped themselves to the vegetables at either end of the table, before animated discussion broke out. It was noisy, but not overbearing. Matisse delighted in teasing Todd, whispering conspiratorially to Sylvie in French. He was more than a little annoyed.

"What gives?" he asked.

"We're talking about you, not to you."

Sylvie moved her head closer to Todd and said something that made him laugh.

"Okay, okay," he told her.

Andrea had made a couple of her famous lemon meringue pies for dessert. They were very well received. The French girl took a mouthful of the topping and looked thoughtfully at Jacob and then at Matisse.

"So, Matisse," she said in French, licking her spoon slowly, "you two are lovers?" She indicated Jacob.

"Pardon. I don't think I understand," Matisse replied, also in French.

"Your French isn't that bad, you understand," Sylvie spoke a little slower.

"What makes you say that?" Matisse asked, referring to the former comment.

"I see the way he looks at you. He would take you to bed now if he could."

"I'm sure you are imagining things."

"I don't think so—there are sparks flying out everywhere. I'm surprised he can keep his hands off you."

"You're crazy."

Jacob caught snatches of the conversation. His French may be rusty, but he understood enough. Matisse was squirming uncomfortably next to him. Todd wasn't the only one getting payback. Sylvie leaned across in front of Matisse to catch his attention.

"Am I right?" she asked boldly in English. Matisse hoped he hadn't heard their conversation. He looked at Matisse for what seemed an eternity, then at Sylvie and back to Matisse.

"Absolutely," he replied slowly. Matisse couldn't breathe and dropped her gaze.

"Ha, I knew it!" Sylvie said triumphantly in English, and turned back to Todd as if nothing had happened.

Matisse suddenly found swallowing hard, and reached for a drink to try and wash the dessert down. She was sure the whole table could hear the pounding of her heart, betraying her.

"Don't look so worried," Jacob whispered. "I gave you my word, remember." She nodded slightly, unconvinced he would actually keep his promise, as he turned to answer a question from his father.

Jacob pushed his seat out from the table, resting his arm across the back of Matisse's chair. She was in total turmoil from the conversation. It didn't help that Jacob was absently rubbing her shoulder with his thumb. He unhurriedly drank his coffee as the others sipped their coffee or tea. Matisse was convinced she was at high risk of spilling anything hot, in her emotional state, so she declined both.

The conversation quietened somewhat until Sam spoke up.

"As soon as the dishes are done, we will be adjourning to the games room for our bi-annual table tennis grudge match. Males versus females," he added, looking at Matisse and Sylvie. "I hope you will agree to join us tonight." Sylvie didn't hesitate. Matisse was less enthusiastic.

With all the extra hands, the kitchen was cleaned up in record time as Sam and Adam talked up their prospects for a good win.

"Don't get too full of it, boys," Mel warned. "For all you know, these two could be champion players."

Adam and Sam just laughed. "We'll see."

THE EXTENDED FAMILY trooped into the large, cosy family room for the game. There was a huge stone fireplace in one corner, perfect for cold winter Cape nights. Along one wall were built-in bookshelves and a cabinet stacked with games, as well as a table smaller than the one in the main house. A casual lounge area nearby had several very comfortable-looking long couches arranged in a U-shape.

The well-worn table tennis table was at the far end.

Numbers were drawn out of a bag to determine playing order. The rules were pretty simple: you win the point, you stay on; you lose, the next player is up.

Molly and Lily were too short to play. They had their own game, standing on chairs with someone behind helping them make the shots.

Then the main game turned serious, or as serious as it could with all the sledging and quips flying back and forth from the sidelines. Claire Davis kept score while her husband was umpire, but he wasn't above being bribed, which added to the hilarity. Matisse couldn't help but admire Jacob as he moved around the room and interacted with his family. On more than one occasion he caught her out watching him. The colour kept rising to her face, but she couldn't look away.

It came time for Matisse to play. Pausing, she put the bat down on the table, took a hair tie out of her pocket, and pulled her hair into a ponytail.

"Oh, watch out boys, this chick means business!"

She positioned herself to receive the serve from Sam. He jokingly tried to psyche her out, but she more than held her own and saw him and Adam off in quick succession, high-fiving their wives as she did so. Unlucky against Todd, she handed her bat over to Andrea, and the game continued at a frantic pace.

They were playing "best of five", and the boys were surprised it was two apiece. The competition amped up a couple of notches.

Match point, and Jake stood opposite her at the other end of the table. There was no way Matisse was even going to look at him. She turned to the team behind her, cheering her on. Serve, rally and it was over. She wasn't sure how she managed to get the ball past Jake, and strongly suspected he'd thrown the point. The other male team members also seemed to suspect as much, but the girls were going crazy, whooping and cheering.

"Well played," he told her over the din. James Davis presented the winning team with the trophy—a gold, spray-painted bat attached to a piece of timber. Mel, as team captain, ribbed the boys mercilessly, which they took in good grace.

As they all moved across to the lounge area at the other end of the room, Matisse slipped outside to grab a breath of fresh air, the noise from the game still ringing in her ears. Sylvie was already there, lighting up a cigarette. Matisse stopped awkwardly —not wanting to talk but not wanting to be rude and walk away. The younger girl drew on the cigarette and blew a cloud of smoke away from Matisse.

Sylvie looked at her. "So, what's holding you back with Jacob?" she wanted to know in her French-accented English.

Matisse was again taken aback by her forthrightness. "My fiancé." Matisse didn't think Sylvie would be easily fobbed off.

"Oh."

"He died two years ago, and I haven't managed to move on."

"Jake is as good a reason as any." She flicked the ash from the end of the cigarette and indicated him through the window.

"It's not that easy."

"Sure, it is. Either you want to sleep with him or you don't. You need to seize him. Vivre la vie."

"Live life?"

"Find some joie de vivre. I'm sure he'd be happy to help you find it again." Sylvie threw the finished cigarette down onto the dirt and ground it out with her booted foot. She walked back inside with a, "Think about it", in French.

After a few minutes trying to process her thoughts Matisse ventured back into the room before someone—Jacob—came looking for her.

Todd and Sylvie were about to leave.

"Thank you for making me feel welcome," Sylvie told the family. "I had fun."

"So, are you staying at the Bayside Backpackers?" Adam asked, referring to a hostel in town.

"No, tonight is my last night, so I think we are going to live it up a bit and stay at Apollo Towers."

"Good choice."

The couple went on their way as the others settled down again. Jacob patted the seat next to him, indicating for Matisse to join him, which was logical seeing as they were "together". Matisse picked her way around the five children sprawled on the floor to join him on the couch. She had hardly sat down when Lily wandered over, climbed into her lap and promptly fell asleep. Matisse eased the little girl into a comfortable position, putting her arms around the sleeping form, content just to sit. Molly followed her cousin's lead and lay down across her parents with her head on her mother's lap. The boys were also fading fast.

"Looks like you have lost your status as favoured grown-up," Adam told Jacob, indicating his daughter.

Jacob shrugged his resignation. "I know, and what's more galling is the fact that man's best friend likes her better, too."

Matisse reminded him about the package they had brought with them, so he went back to the main house to retrieve it, then handed the parcel to his mother.

"Hope you both like it. It's a Reynolds original." He smiled at Matisse.

Claire Davis untied the string and her husband helped rip off the brown paper. Matisse couldn't see their reaction behind the framed canvas. Jacob took the artwork from them and stepped back a couple of paces so they could get a better view. They were both silent, taking in the painting of Pembroke.

Jacob's mother scooped up the paper from the floor and scrunched it up. Getting to her feet, she came over to Matisse.

"It's beautiful, Matisse, thank you so much." She sat down next to the artist and kissed her cheek, then put a hand on the younger woman's arm as Jacob turned the painting around for the others to view. The girls gave a collective gasp. Sam whistled appreciatively.

"Awesome job there, Matisse," Adam told her.

"Matisse was brave enough to allow me to have it framed."

"You chose well," Matisse admitted, as he took the artwork over to the mantelpiece and propped it up. There was some discussion about the most appropriate place to hang the painting —by the front door, the dining room, the drawing room—but no consensus was reached.

"Anyway," Adam announced, getting up, "I think it's about time we made tracks." He rounded up the sleepy Ashton.

Mel came over to Matisse, but Jacob waved her away. "I'll take Lily."

He locked eyes with Matisse as he reached to move his niece. She was sure his eyes told her, "This could be us." But maybe she was mistaken. As he lifted the little girl, she stirred long enough to wrap her arms around his neck and settle her head on his shoulder. Matisse felt her insides turn to mush at the tender sight.

"CAN YOU GRAB HER BAG?" Jacob asked. Matisse got down on the floor and gathered the art supplies and scattered bits and pieces, sorting them under Andrea's direction from where she sat with Molly.

"Goodnight Dad. 'Night Mum. Don't come out. Thanks for dinner." Mel hugged her parents.

James planted a kiss on his sleeping granddaughter as Jacob carried her out. He followed his sister across the courtyard and through the gateway to their four-wheel drive. Mel opened the back door and Jake manoeuvred Lily into her seat, while her mother fastened the seatbelt. Matisse put the bag on the floor at Lily's feet.

Matisse didn't seem to mind when Jacob put an arm around

her waist, leaning into him briefly as they watched Adam drive off with the family.

They'd only walked back as far as the gate when Jacob decided to steal a kiss. The only trouble was, one was never going to be enough. He steadied her against the wall and kissed her deeply as her hands wound themselves around his neck. A small groan of pleasure escaped her lips as his hands roamed over her, slipping under the edge of her blouse as it rode up. His hands stroked the soft skin of her back—the flame of desire was almost burning out of control.

"Sylvie was right," he murmured between kisses, "I can't keep my hands off you."

He wasn't the only one having trouble keeping hands off. Matisse had tugged his shirt free from the waistband so she could run her hands over his chest and around his back. He groaned her name, her touch threatening to buckle his knees.

They were hungry for each other. He sucked her bottom lip into his mouth before dipping his tongue in to taste her. She returned the favour. Matisse sighed, fingers in his hair as he kissed a hot trail down the open neckline of her shirt. Jake reached the chain. The pendant moved. She suddenly pulled out of his arms and put some distance between them, fingering the chain.

Jacob palmed the wall heavily in frustration. One second, she was melting in his arms and the next, she'd slipped out of his embrace. He was sure she was trembling with desire even though she refused to look at him. She wanted him as much as he wanted her. He wanted to rip the damn chain off her neck. But that would be taking a huge risk.

Instead, he turned away from her as he smoothed his shirt and re-tucked it into his waistband, allowing his breathing to return to normal. Matisse rearranged herself, then hurried back through the gate, crossing the courtyard with Jacob striding to keep up.

Andi and Sam appeared at the doorway with their three.

"Time for us to head off as well."

"Same," Jacob told them. They said their goodbyes as James and Claire followed behind.

"Thanks for the lovely dinner," Matisse told them. "I enjoyed the night."

"You must come again," Claire told her, as both she and James gave her a peck on the cheek.

Following Andrea and Sam's car out, Jacob then turned off in the other direction toward home. He set an instrumental CD in motion to fill the silence in the Ranger. By the time he pulled up at the cabin, he was annoyed. She hadn't said a word to him the entire time. The passenger's side door opened.

He decided to ask the question even though he knew the answer. "Stay with me tonight?"

She wouldn't look at him, and shook her head as she unbuckled the seatbelt and slid out of the car. There was a back-ward glance, but she kept going. Jacob watched every step until she closed the cabin door. He desperately wanted to follow her, to make her see reason, but he thought better of it. He kept reminding himself that she needed to come to him. Maybe if he repeated it often enough, he would believe it. He slammed his hand on the steering wheel and shoved the car into gear. He was going to need a long, cold shower.

Matisse dropped her clothes in a heap on the floor. Every part of her that he'd touched still tingled.

She lay on the stretcher, full of regret. Why had she pulled away? She'd felt so alive again, and yet something ... or maybe someone ... was still holding her back from committing herself fully to Jacob. If the truth be known, she was scared a relation-ship with Jacob would eclipse what she'd had with Jonno. She thought what she'd experienced with Jonno was everything she wanted, but she realised with Jacob she was on a whole other level. Was she disrespecting Jonno's memory?

Sleep was elusive.

At first light, Matisse hauled herself out of bed and automatically picked up a paintbrush.

But everything was wrong.

No matter how many times she tried she just couldn't get the right shade of colour.

Arghh!

Paint tubes hit the wall in a satisfying release of pent-up emotion.

Clomping around the confined space was not helping.

The creek.

She bolted down the back steps and headed for the seat, pulling her legs up, wrapping her arms around her knees, pressing her cheek against the top of her knees.

Breathe. In. Out.

Repeat.

Don't think about him.

Just. Don't ...

Her state of mind in the following days was splashed across a blank canvas. Then another, and another. The only way Matisse coped was to immerse herself in artwork. She worked at a frantic pace. She supposed she should thank Jacob. He made himself scarce. Missing him wasn't an option she could afford at the moment.

CHAPTER SIXTEEN

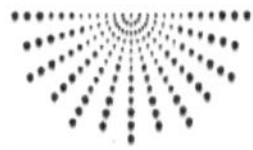

$\mathcal{M}$atisse took a final walk around the gallery with Max and Diedre ahead of the official opening. She was more anxious than she had been for any previous exhibition. Max took Matisse's arm to reassure her.

"Thanks Max." She patted his arm. "I appreciate your confidence. I'm rather nervous coming back after all this time away."

"Don't worry, you will be a huge success as always."

Matisse gazed at her reflection in the full-length bedroom mirror at the Bondi apartment. The hairstylist had done her job and Matisse was pleased enough. Makeup—check. She brushed her hands over the dress chosen for her to wear, unsure if it was a wise choice. She sighed, not entirely comfortable and hoping she could pull it off. Once in a while it was fine to dress up—and this was her once in a while. She owed it to Max to present the polished look he asked of her. It was only for one night, after all. It was the very least she could do.

Dee would not be joining them. Not with all the people that would be crowding into the gallery space tonight. She pulled Matisse in for a quick hug before waving her off. "Good luck, my dear. I'll be waiting to hear how it goes."

JAKE USUALLY ESCHEWED WEARING A SUIT, but tonight was black tie. He pulled at his collar as the driver of his hired limo pulled up at the nondescript red brick building tucked away in a back street of the Sydney CBD on the edge of The Rocks.

He hadn't seen Matisse in almost three weeks, and wasn't sure he'd made a wise decision to come, but he was more than a little keen to see her artwork. He had deliberately chosen to arrive late, to hopefully avoid media scrutiny.

Showing his invitation at the door, he slipped in at the back just as Matisse took to the stage to a warm round of applause. At least, he assumed it was Matisse. She looked so different tonight, like she had just stepped off the red carpet at a movie premiere in London or New York. The figure-hugging pastel green dress had a low-cut neckline with three-quarter sleeves. She was wearing a heap of jewellery bling that matched her eyes. His heart rate amped up a few notches. He couldn't take his eyes off her.

The man he had seen coming out of the hotel with her—Max, her agent—spoke about the accident and her rehab and the paintings on display. Matisse made a short speech, thanking everyone for coming—not that he could remember much else of what she said over the pounding of his heart in his ears. Matisse praised Max, and couldn't speak highly enough of his support in getting her through the last couple of years. Jake felt that stab of jealousy again as she hugged and kissed the older man.

Were they, or not? He couldn't be sure, one way or the other.

There was a ripple of recognition nearby and he steeled himself for the inevitable attention.

MATISSE WAS TALKING to an older Canadian couple who were gushing over one of her artworks when she caught sight of Jake and momentarily lost her train of thought. She hadn't been brave enough to check the guest list, in case. But there he was. Devastatingly handsome in a black suit, Jacob seemed to be attracting attention—not that she was surprised.

Excusing herself, she made a beeline for him, but got waylaid and lost sight of his figure. Max took her arm and introduced her to a group of people who were supporters of the gallery. Patrons, some of them. She knew the drill, and turned on the charm. It wasn't something she particularly enjoyed but if it helped to sell more paintings, then it would help both the hospital and school she supported in Bali.

JAKE WAS WANDERING, glass in hand, around the display of paintings. Many of them already sported the red "sold" dot on the attached description. An attendant added a couple more stickers to paintings as he stood there.

There were three distinct sections. One part was an obvious Bali theme—older paintings he assumed were "before". The second section were the dark ones, as Matisse struggled with the aftermath of her accident. Then there were the more recent ones with the Great Ocean Road features predominant, including three sunrise paintings featuring the Apostles, inspired no doubt by their early morning sojourn. All sold.

There were definite similarities between those paintings and John Russell's from Belle ... wherever it was. Not that he'd tell her. He remembered she hated the comparisons. Seeing all the artwork on display reminded him how hugely talented she was, and how fortunate he was that she ended up staying in the cabin on his property.

Matisse finally worked her way around to him. The full-out assault on his senses from her perfume as she stepped next to him scrambled his brain. "Jake. So glad you could make it."

He wanted to kiss her. Badly. But he wouldn't dream of

doing that here. In public. Instead, he squashed the feeling down and raised his glass at the room in general. "Very impressive turn out," he told her.

She glanced around, seeming to take it all in. "Yes, it is."

"You should be proud of yourself for getting this exhibition up."

Jake took in her sleek and sophisticated look. He was having a hard time breathing. She was drop-dead gorgeous and he had to stop himself from reaching out and tugging her hair loose from the updo she was wearing so he could tangle his fingers in its thickness and ... he stopped himself and shoved his free hand into his pocket as his eyes flicked briefly down to the low neckline. There was no sign of Jonno's pendant tonight.

"Thanks, it's very encouraging, although a lot of people are here for the curiosity factor."

"Curious or not, they seem to be buying up big."

"Hopefully I will be able to make a significant donation to Bali."

"I was surprised you didn't make mention of it in your speech."

Matisse shook her head. "It's just a private thing that I don't really want publicised. I prefer to keep it low-key in case it raises too many questions."

Jacob was all too aware of keeping things low-key. The words were hardly out of her mouth when a photographer turned up at her elbow to request a picture. Jake moved to back out of the way, but the photographer insisted and pulled another couple into the shot. While she was busy fussing with her camera, Jake managed to discreetly move away from Matisse and put the other couple in between. He didn't want the risk of unnecessary publicity if he was associated with Matisse. Their relationship was still in its early days, and he'd had media attention damage relationships in the past. So now his private life was private, and he protected it fiercely. He knew he was taking a risk being here, let alone being in close proximity to Matisse or any other woman in the room for that matter. He had already been quizzed by a reporter, and hoped he'd been able to fob her off. Eventually the photographer moved off and after exchanging a few pleasantries the other couple drifted away.

Jake heard an audible gasp. "Oh, my."

"Anything wrong?"

"See that women over there with Max?" He followed her gaze to a short middle-aged woman with short dark hair, wearing a black and red patterned dress.

"What about her?"

"That's Jonno's aunt." She glanced around furtively, but Jake stopped her escape.

"I think you should talk to her."

"No, I can't," she pleaded.

"Can't or won't? You should make an effort. It can't have been easy for her to turn up here. She must want to connect with you." She gulped as Jake took her elbow and steered her over to where Max was talking.

Max turned to Matisse with obvious concern about how she would react. "Matisse. You remember Sarah McDonald-Reid?" She went to shake hands with the woman and was unexpectedly caught up in a hug.

"Matisse, it's lovely to see you."

Jake spoke to Max quietly. "Maybe there's somewhere more private to talk?"

"Of course." Max ushered them out to his office. Matisse threw Jacob a "don't you dare leave me" look, so he followed along. Max excused himself as soon as he let them into the room. Jake walked behind the two women into the office. It was a spacious room with a magnificent timber desk to one side, and matching bookcases. The decor was minimalist. There were several recessed niches around the walls displaying various artwork, carefully lit to show them to their full advantage. Jacob could recognise at least one as belonging to Matisse, and maybe a second as well. He walked over and glanced at the corner of the canvas, looking for her telltale signature. Yes, it was one of hers.

"Can I get either of you ladies a drink of some sort?"

Sarah turned to him. "Sorry, I don't believe we've met?"

He took her outstretched hand. "Jake," he replied, without adding any more information other than, "I'm a friend of Matisse."

"Pleased to meet you. I could actually go a coffee if that's possible? White with one."

"I'll see what I can do. Matisse?" He looked at her, but she shook her head. Heading to the small kitchenette adjacent to the office, Jacob took his time making the drink.

MATISSE INDICATED for Sarah to sit down on one of the large chairs in the corner sitting area.

"Jake seems a nice guy," Sarah told the younger woman.

"He's been a godsend the last couple of months, to be honest. I've been down near Cape Otway since August. He lives in the area." Matisse wasn't about to reveal too much to Jonno's aunt, so she changed the subject. "I'm curious to know how you ended up here tonight."

"Max invited me," Sarah confessed before continuing, "I've actually been in contact with him on a regular basis since the accident."

"You have?"

Sarah nodded. "I didn't want to bother you. I wasn't sure you would even want to hear from me. I just wanted to know how you were going ... and how are you going, Matisse?"

"The last couple of years have been tough, really tough. I think I can see a light at the end of the tunnel, but I'm not sure. I've really only started painting again in the last few months. Before that ..." she shrugged as she trailed off.

~

MATISSE DIDN'T TAKE any notice of Jake as he returned with the coffee and set it down on the table in front of Sarah, retreating to the background as Sarah leaned forward in her seat. "Matisse, do you mind if I ask about the night of the accident? I would like to know, and I'm sure it would help Jonathan's parents."

Jacob watched as Matisse took a deep breath. "There's not a lot to tell. We went out to dinner. Our six-month anniversary." Matisse was staring down at her hands clenched in her lap. "It was the restaurant where we first met. And, well, after dinner, he proposed."

"He did?"

Matisse nodded, smiling at the memory. "He got down on one knee in the middle of the restaurant and produced a ring ..."

"Go on," Sarah prompted.

"Well, I said yes. We celebrated with a drink and a long walk along the beach. Then we went to go home. Jonno was driving the scooter. He wasn't wearing a helmet—he never wore one, and always teased me for wearing mine ... we started to leave the restaurant ... I think we were about halfway home .... I'm sorry, I don't remember anything after that. According to the police report we were hit by a drunk driver who fled the scene. Some bystanders tried to give chase, but he got away and was never caught. The next thing, I woke up in hospital a few days later. Max was there, he'd flown in from Sydney. He was the one who told me Jonno hadn't survived ... We were officially engaged for about ... an hour and a half, I guess. Life and living just got a whole lot tougher from then on. Once I was stable enough, I was flown back here to hospital in Australia. I really struggled, physically and mentally. The physical injuries healed soon enough. I was in hospital a couple of months. But mentally I was in a dark place for a very long time ..."

Jacob could hear the anguish in her voice and desperately

wanted to hold her and tell her it was okay, but he stayed where he was.

"And now?"

"I'm living the best I can. I have bad days and good ones. Lately I think the good ones are starting to outweigh the bad." She glanced up at Jake and gave him a half smile. "I wondered if I could ever find a place of happiness again. If I hadn't been able to paint, I'm not sure where I'd be, although I admit it was many months before I was even able to look at a paintbrush, let alone pick one up and put it to use." She paused and then asked, "What about Jonno's parents? How are you all going?"

"As well as can be expected, I guess. His brother Steven and his wife had a baby about eight months ago, a boy, Liam Jonathan. He's helped ease some of the pain and given them something else to focus their attention on. They set up the Jonathan Reid Foundation in his memory."

"Yes, I know. I actually sent them a donation, but it got returned. Something about not taking outside money, but I suspect that's not quite true."

"Matisse, I'm sorry. I never realised."

"I think that's been the hardest thing. To have had a relationship with Jonno, to the point of being engaged, but not having anything, not even my existence, acknowledged by his parents."

"I know, Matisse, I've actually tried several times to get them to make contact with you."

"You did?"

Sarah nodded, taking a sip of her coffee. "But they refused. I guess they blame you for the accident."

"I blame myself too, don't worry."

"You shouldn't, Matisse. Jonno chose not to wear the helmet."

"I know, but he wasn't supposed to still be in Bali, remember. He should have been back home, working in the family business."

"You didn't force him to stay. He chose to stay with you in Bali. To be honest, he wasn't thrilled about working in the business." She paused while she drank some more coffee and looked at the younger woman thoughtfully. "Matisse, Jonno wouldn't want to see you like this. You need to live again. I know that the time Jonno had with you was the happiest and most content I'd ever seen him." Matisse was staring at the floor biting her lip.

"I hope in time you might find someone else ..." Sarah glanced up at Jacob with a raised eyebrow. He was leaning back on the corner of Max's desk, arms and legs crossed, giving nothing away, "... to love as much as you loved Jonno ... or even more."

SHORTLY AFTERWARD, Sarah moved to leave. Jacob walked her out to the gallery to give Matisse some breathing space.

"Have you known Matisse long—Jake, isn't it?"

"We just met a couple of months back."

"Has she told you much about Jonno?"

"Just the basics, really." He got the feeling he was about to find out more.

"Jonno was the quintessential bronzed Aussie surfing larrikin. He lived to chase the waves, much to his parents' frustration at times. As soon as he could after school, he left to travel and surf. Eventually, his parents pinned him down to do a business degree. It was a long drawn-out process—the lure of the perfect wave was often too much to resist." She smiled. "But he could charm anyone. Charmed his way through life really. After finishing uni, he and his mates celebrated by heading to Bali for a three-month surfing holiday. Which, of course, is where he met Matisse. Things quickly got serious between them. At the end of the three months the other guys came back to Australia and Jonno stayed on with her. He was due to start a job in the family business, so when he didn't come back, it didn't go down too well. To find out he'd moved in with an older woman—an artist, no less—well, that really set the cat amongst the pigeons. His older brother was despatched to bring him back, but that failed. He was even threatened with disinheritance, but Jonno stuck to his guns. I'd always had a soft spot for Jonno, so I decided to go and check out the situation for myself. I stayed for about a week. They were so happy and so in love. I was thrilled for Jonno and put in a good word for Matisse with his parents when I got back. They were sure it was just a holiday fling and that he'd eventually come to his senses and return home. I'm not sure why they were so antagonistic towards someone they'd never met, but I was equally convinced that given some time and the chance to meet Matisse, they would come around. But sadly, they never got the opportunity, and now they are just not interested in knowing anything about her. They have never expressed any concern for Matisse, or her welfare, and they went to extraordinary lengths to keep the details out of the media."

Jacob's head was spinning from the information that Sarah was divulging.

"I, on the other hand, have been desperate for any snippets of information I could get. I've followed her progress via the media and got in contact with Max once she returned home, and have stayed in touch with him on a regular basis since then. I've waited a long time to find out what she remembers about the accident. I know that Jonno was supremely happy—they both were. I can only hope that one day Matisse might find love and happiness again. I think that's the least she deserves." She looked up at Jacob, but he kept his expression guarded.

"I appreciate you confiding in me. Matisse hasn't said much, so it helps to know a bit more about what she has been going through."

"Well, you seem a nice enough young man. Make sure you look after her, you hear?"

He could only nod as she left. There was such a lot of information for him to digest. As he walked back across the gallery, past a row of paintings, one caught his eye. Jacob wasn't sure why he hadn't noticed it before. Stopping to take a closer look, he recognised the logging cabin and its surrounds. It was impressive, and surprisingly not yet sold. He made a spur of the moment decision to buy it, and immediately knew where he would hang it in his house.

~

IT TOOK a while to complete the paperwork and when he got back to Matisse, she wasn't alone. Max was holding her as she dabbed her eyes with a tissue. Jacob couldn't stop the stab of jealousy he felt that another man was holding her. The older man turned to Jacob as he stood in the doorway and came over to him while Matisse turned her back and wrapped her arms around herself.

"I was wondering if you would mind taking Matisse home. I think she has had about enough for one night."

Jacob nodded. "Of course."

"You can go out the back door. There's still too many people wandering around to take her through the gallery."

Jacob reached for his phone to alert his driver.

"It's Baxter Lane," Max informed him. "I'd better get back, thanks, um, Jake. Why don't you come around for lunch tomorrow? Dee would love to meet you."

"Dee?"

"Deidre, my wife."

"Okay."

"Let's say around one?" Max stretched his hand out for Jacob and then handed over Matisse's clutch purse as he left the office. Matisse hadn't moved. Jake loosened his tie and shoved it in his coat pocket as he stepped close to her.

"I assume you know the way out of here?" She nodded and he followed her, away from the muffled gallery noise, along a narrow hallway and down a set of stairs. A cool breeze enveloped them as she pushed the door open. Matisse shivered. Jacob automatically took his suit jacket off and wrapped it around her shoulders, opening the car door when the limo glided up to the kerb.

Relaying the address, Jacob stretched his arm across the back of the seat and Matisse moved over to lean up against him and put her hand against his chest, which he covered with his free hand.

"I forgot to mention, you look absolutely amazing tonight." She nodded her thanks.

He enjoyed having her nestled up against him. He breathed in her perfume as he rested his cheek against the top of her hair and gently massaged the top of her arm. She was so quiet on the thirty-minute trip to Bondi, he was sure she was asleep. When the car pulled up at the Campbell Parade apartment, Matisse stirred.

"C'mon, I'll walk you in." He held her elbow as he guided her up the half a dozen steps to the frosted glass entry. She reached into her purse for a set of keys and touched the fob to the security point next to the door. When the light turned green, Jacob pulled down the handle, swinging the door open for her. In the elevator, she swiped the key again and hit the button for the top floor penthouse suite. Stifling a yawn as the lift opened, Matisse led the way to the nearby door.

Turning to Jake, she apologised. "Sorry I've been a bit quiet. Tonight turned out to be more overwhelming than expected."

"It's okay, I understand."

Closing the gap between them, she shrugged out of his jacket and handed it back, waiting while he slipped it on.

"Thanks, I appreciate your understanding and for coming in the first place. It meant a lot to me ... especially being there with Jonno's aunt."

He thought his response of, "You're welcome," seemed rather inadequate.

Her kiss wasn't totally unexpected, but the intensity took

him by surprise. He held back, knowing she was tired and vulnerable in that moment. But he made the fatal mistake of looking into her beautiful eyes and he was sunk. He couldn't help himself.

He groaned her name and pulled her hard up against him, and tried to find the line to walk with her. Her bare shoulder caught his attention and she trembled at the onslaught of kisses he feathered against her skin. Eventually, calling a halt, he unwrapped her arms from around his neck, then bent to retrieve her purse from where it had fallen on the ground. He took the keys from her fingers and tapped them against the red light, waiting for the click, then opened the door.

"I'll see you for lunch in a few hours." He pushed her gently inside the door and turned to go.

Jacob had difficulty sleeping. He kept running the name McDonald-Reid—Jonno's aunt—through his mind. Initially, the name escaped him, but then he remembered. Reid. Reid Transport and Logistics, from Western Australia.

He got up and flicked on his laptop. He did an internet search and scrolled through the information about Jonno's family. His parents appeared on the screen. His brother and sister, but no Jonno. There was a family photo—also no Jonathan. After a bit of digging he came across an interview which mentioned Jonathan had died overseas in an accident, but that was about the extent of it. Any attempts by the reporter to find out any more information had obviously been comprehensively stonewalled.

There were a couple of articles alluding to rumours of death by misadventure in Bali. But the family maintained its right to privacy, and it seemed they even took out an injunction against the television network and its affiliates that had dug around, to prevent them from broadcasting anything.

Eventually, he discovered an image of Jonathan Reid and clicked on it. He found it remarkable in this day and age that there was so little about him on the internet. This was the man that Matisse was engaged to, if only briefly, with his blond, curly hair and blue eyes. Definitely the typical laidback bronzed Aussie surfer type. Jacob felt his blood boil at the thought of another man, this man, being intimate with Matisse. He didn't know why he should be so jealous. It wasn't like he expected she'd lived a chaste lifestyle. Heck he hadn't exactly been celibate his whole life either.

He blew a breath out. He was in way too deep with Matisse. He knew it and didn't care. The pull she had on him was overwhelmingly strong. It was becoming impossible for him to imagine a future without her.

But he wasn't sure she was over Jonno. He would keep trying to convince her, but he didn't think she was ready to give her heart to him just yet. He knew it would be well worth the wait.

Matisse, on the other hand, had hold of his heart a long time ago.

CHAPTER SEVENTEEN

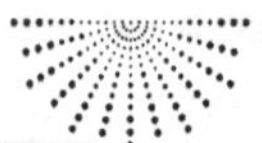

Soon enough, Jacob was back in the foyer of the Bondi apartment block. There were only two apartments on each of five floors, and the penthouse suite. He buzzed, and waited for someone to come down in the lift. He hoped it would be Matisse who stepped out, but it was Max Stanard who greeted him.

Jacob shook hands with the older man as he walked into the elevator. "So, how do you think the opening went last night?" Jacob inquired.

"Good—there's only a couple of works left unsold, and I expect they will be gone before too long."

"How's Matisse doing today?"

"Didn't sleep all that well, so she's pretty tired. The meeting with Sarah was draining. Having to relive everything again. But she's doing better than expected. I wondered if you might have something to do with that." Fortunately, the elevator door opened at that moment and Max exited without waiting for a reply.

Jacob was unsure how to greet Matisse after the passion of the night before, but he needn't have worried. Wearing a sleeveless blue maxi dress that floated around her, she walked over and gave him a light kiss on the cheek. She looked tired, but her smile melted him all the same as she took his arm and led him across the room.

The penthouse Max and his wife lived in was expansive and predominantly white, contrasting beautifully with the blue Pacific vista that could be seen from anywhere in the living areas via floor-to-ceiling glass, giving it a "beach house" feel. Large white floor tiles ran through the living areas. The oversized, soft grey lounge was inviting with its huge matching cushions. The seats faced a floating white storage unit with a television attached to the wall above. A white coffee table held a shallow, hand-blown, red, fluted glass bowl that dominated the surface. Underneath, the rug consisted of large squares of carpet in alternating colours of grey and sand with the occasional punch of red.

"Come on, I want you to meet Dee."

Deidre Stanard was a strikingly elegant woman of medium height with a slim build. She reminded Jake of the former Australian Governor-General, Dame Quentin Bryce. Everything about her was immaculate: the greying hair in a short bob; the white trousers and pink-toned kaftan top. The matching pink-polished fingers that reached out to shake his hand held a myriad of rings and bracelets.

"Jacob, so lovely to finally meet you. Matisse has given you a favourable review." She kissed his cheek, a charming hostess. "We're going to eat out on the balcony. I hope you don't mind."

Jacob followed Deidre and Matisse across the lounge area and out the huge sliding doors. He paused to take in the impressive sight south across the cream sand of the iconic Bondi Beach, from the bathing pavilion all the way up to the white Icebergs Swimming Club building with its bathing pools, perched on the cliff side almost directly opposite.

"You have an amazing view," he commented, sitting where Dee indicated.

"Yes, it is rather special, but I hear the view where you live is equally spectacular."

"You heard correctly. My home overlooks Bass Strait, not far from the Lightstation at Cape Otway."

"Matisse mentioned you grew up in the area."

"My parents' property is about twenty minutes' drive away. My place originally belonged to a childhood friend, so I spent a lot of time there growing up." He was handed a platter of cold cut meats to serve himself as he answered the question.

"Can I get you a drink, Jake?" Max asked.

"No, I'm fine. I rarely drink alcohol these days. I gave it a good go in my early twenties, but decided it caused too much trouble. A uni friend went to jail for a hit-and-run accident. He was drunk at the time."

"So, what do you do for a living?"

Jacob's response was guarded. "I have several business interests, the main one being a tour company I run out of Apollo Bay. We do walking tours of the Great Ocean Road and that sort of thing. We have our own accommodation, and run several helicopters for scenic flights up and down the coast and for charter work."

"What type of choppers do you use?"

"Robinson." There was some discussion about the merits of various types of helicopters. Max was surprisingly knowledgeable on the subject.

Jake had hoped that would be enough to satisfy their curiosity without having to reveal more until he got to know them.

"What family do you have, Jake?" Dee took the salad bowl from him and passed it on.

"Well, I have two sisters, one older and one younger. Both married with kids. Andi ... Andrea and Sam help my parents run the accommodation on the property. They also live there. Mum and Dad are still in the original homestead. Andi and Sam have built a new place nearby. They have three kids. My younger sister Melanie and her husband Adam live in Apollo Bay. They have a motel with a gift shop slash art gallery attached. Mel still finds time to fit in a couple of nursing shifts at the hospital. Adam is also an SES volunteer. They have two kids. Then there's the baby of the family, Todd—the surprise package, if you will. I was thirteen when he was born. He's usually busy backpacking his way around the world, but he's home at the moment because he ran out of money, so he'll work a few months and undoubtedly take off again."

Thankfully their interest turned to other matters. As the conversation ebbed and flowed, Jacob could see how relaxed Matisse was and how fond of her the Stanards were. She laughed often, which he hadn't heard much of in the time he'd known her, and he loved the sound of her enjoying herself.

"Looks like we could do with some more water." Matisse excused herself and wandered inside.

Jacob seized the initiative as soon as she was out of earshot.

"So how long have you known Matisse?"

"Jenny, Matisse's mum, worked as a cleaner at the gallery," Max said. "She was a single mum and approached me one day when Matisse was about fifteen with a portfolio of her artwork. She wanted to know if her daughter was as talented as she thought, or if it was just a mother's pride in her little girl. I liked what I saw. Dee and I decided to help support her through high school and uni. Her mum came to work as our housekeeper, and we found them an apartment within walking distance. Matisse won a scholarship to study in Paris and then had plans to stay on, but her mother got sick and she decided to come home. She took over from her mum, worked a couple more jobs while painting on the side, and looked after her mother until she passed away. If she hadn't already been old enough, we would have signed up to become her legal guardians. We were never able to have our own family. Matisse is like a daughter to us."

"Not to mention you've done okay on commission from my artwork," Matisse teased, as she came back with the refilled jug.

"That too," he acknowledged with a laugh, patting her arm as she took the seat next to him.

The realisation that he had totally misjudged the relationship between Matisse and Max hit Jacob hard. He was disgusted with himself for even daring to think there was anything untoward going on. Jealous? He wasn't usually the type. But Matisse affected him in ways he was only still coming to terms with.

They all helped clear the table. Jacob would have none of "the guest doesn't help with the clean-up". They congregated in the large galley kitchen space with its limed wood cabinetry and kept talking, mostly comparing travel stories. Like Jacob, Max and Dee had travelled extensively, so conversation was easy.

"Matisse, why don't you show Jacob around?"

"Okay, come on then." She stretched off the bench where she had been leaning and led the way.

Jacob followed, slowing to a stop to take in the photographs on the wall. An assortment of Max and Dee from their various travels, interspersed with Matisse at her high school formal, uni graduation and in Paris. There were several artworks in the apartment. Not all of them by Matisse, but one drew his attention. He realised it was Deidre. Matisse had captured her understated elegance very well.

Matisse apologised. "My portraiture still needs work. I'm not quite up to Archibald standards yet," she said, referring to the prestigious art competition.

"Sorry, I don't agree, but I'll have to take your word for it." They toured the apartment and ended back with Max and Dee. Jacob made to leave and Matisse walked him to the door.

"Have you any plans for tonight?" he said.

"Not yet."

"I'd like to take you out for dinner."

"Oh, that would be nice."

"I'll give you a call a bit later to let you know a time. I've a couple of business things to attend to and I'm not sure yet how long they will take."

"Sure, I understand."

"No need to see me out."

Jake made several phone calls to organise the evening and was well pleased with the results.

WHEN MATISSE EMERGED from the apartment block early that evening, she found Jacob waiting, arms crossed, leaning back against the side of a black Audi limo. He wore tan chinos and matching shoes, as well as a light blue shirt and navy blazer. Gorgeous. There was no other word for him.

Her skin tingled as he put his hand lightly on her back, exposed by the black halter-neck jumpsuit she was wearing, as he guided her into the car.

"YOU'LL JUST HAVE to wait and see," Jacob replied to her question when he joined her in the limo. Her hair was pulled back in a high ponytail. If he leaned in closer to her, he could catch a tantalising trace of the perfume she was wearing. His hand brushed hers. Then he laced their fingers. She gave a small sigh and settled back in the seat.

Matisse was nonplussed when they eventually pulled up at a side entrance to the Art Gallery of New South Wales.

"What's this all about?"

"Come on," he told her. The door wasn't locked as they made their way into the building. His hand automatically went to her waist.

The gallery director was waiting and shook hands with Jacob.

"Thanks for accommodating us at such short notice."

"You're welcome. You must be Matisse. It's a pleasure to meet you. I understand you are a previous recipient of one of our scholarships."

Matisse fell into step beside him as they walked through the gallery space. "That was about ten years ago."

"I believe we have one of your paintings in our Australian Artists in Paris Collection."

They walked down the short flight of stairs together. The wall signage in front of them announced the Archibald Prize.

"I'm sure you will enjoy your own private tour," the director continued. "Your timing is good. We are just about to start preparing the paintings to take the exhibition on its regional tour."

"How many entries did you receive this year?" Matisse wanted to know.

"Well over eight hundred."

Her hand swept the room as they walked through the doorway. "I don't envy you the task of choosing the finalists."

THE DIRECTOR LED them over to the first of the artworks chosen to hang in this year's exhibition. Matisse was quickly engrossed in the stories of the artists and the background of the paintings. She almost seemed to forget Jacob was there. Not that he minded—he was happy to take a backseat.

When he recognised the People's Choice award, he made a comment which drew her attention to him. Matisse reached out and put her hand on his elbow, pulling him in closer to her side to include him in the conversation. There was some spirited discussion.

Jacob was fascinated by how animated Matisse had become during the course of their time in the exhibit. He was learning a lot about painting. He could relate to the piece chosen by the packing room workers as the recipient of their own particular prize. The overall winner wasn't so much to his liking, but he appreciated the work involved in producing an art piece of that magnitude.

The trio continued through the rooms, examining the finalists of the Sulman and Wynne Prizes for genre painting and Australian landscape respectively, that were awarded at the same time as the Archibald.

Matisse thanked the director profusely for allowing them a private viewing as he ushered them out some time later.

Matisse clutched Jacob's arm as she chatted, her eyes shining as they made their way back to the car. He smiled, looking down at her as she explained something to him. He had no idea what she was actually saying, he was just focused on her face, those eyes and ... her lips. She was so kissable.

But before he could close the gap between them, Matisse stretched up and planted a sweet kiss on him. "Thank you for organising that, Jacob. I really enjoyed it."

"I can tell. You're very welcome." He settled her in the car and came around the other side and joined her, signalling to the driver to continue the journey.

"Now what?"

"Now we have dinner." Jacob's limousine driver took them to one of hotels near Circular Quay. The restaurant on level thirty-six had a small room tucked away just for the two of them. A white starched tablecloth held a centrepiece of pale red orchids resting on a rectangular mirror. Tealights in small opaque votive holders bounced light off the glassware alongside larger clear bubble bowls.

Outside the picture windows, the Opera House at the end of the quay was magical. The distinctive white curves of the roof sails lit up the night. To the left, the Harbour Bridge was equally stunning. Tonight, the lights were blue and the pylons at either end were bathed in a pale yellow glow.

"You certainly know the best places to eat," she told him between mouthfuls of the smoked duck breast she had chosen as a starter. "This is good, Jacob."

"I admit I have a weakness for fine dining—which is why I need a gym at home," he told her. "It gets a good work-out, especially after I've been overseas."

"So, tell me, do you have tried and tested restaurants, or are you one for exploring culinary establishments?"

"Both, actually. I usually have a favourite restaurant in most of the places I visit on a regular basis, but I also go exploring when I get the chance. You find some out of the way gems— especially if you choose to eat where the locals eat, not the tourists."

"Favourite country?"

"Hmmm. No can do," he told her. "Apart from Australia, which has the best of everything. I've spent a lot of time in New Zealand and Fiji, so they are high on the list. But honestly, there's usually one or two places in every country I've been to that are favourites, some I've been fortunate to go back to." He decided to broach the subject. "So, you said Jonno's aunt visited you in Bali ..."

"Yes, not long after his brother had delivered an ultimatum from their parents." Matisse didn't look up, continuing to eat. "She came for about a week. We got on okay, I guess. At least she wasn't as antagonistic as Michael had been."

"Any idea why he was like that?"

Matisse shrugged. "He made it clear that Jonathan was to go back to Australia, to the family business, otherwise he would be disinherited. I think Jonno may have played around in the past and caused a bit of trouble, and the family had had enough and wanted to call him to heel. Anyway, Jonathan refused to entertain any notion of going back. The threat of losing his inheritance had worked before, but not this time ..."

Jacob waited in silence. He could tell she had more to say but was in two minds about it.

"I never told Jonno, but Michael got me on my own and tried to pay me off to break up with his brother. Michael wasn't impressed that I turned the offer down. He thought I was holding out for more money, which he duly offered. He was absolutely convinced I was nothing more than a gold digger. I didn't know initially that Jonathan was from a well-to-do family. By the time I did, I was too far gone. If I had known earlier, I probably wouldn't have gotten involved."

"Because?"

"I'm just not into money and the power and corruption that inevitably go with it."

Jacob wasn't sure he liked where this was heading. "You say it like it's a foregone conclusion."

"I've seen it enough times in my life to know I don't want a part of it. If I'd had any doubts beforehand, Jonathan's family sealed the deal for me."

"What about Max and Dee? They're not exactly working class."

"There's money and there's money."

"What about all the philanthropic pursuits?" He felt the need to justify himself—to both Matisse and himself.

"It seems most of them only donate a small portion of their wealth to appease their conscience. Some make a big show of what they do."

"I think you'll find a lot of people donate on the quiet, like you do, preferring not to make a big deal of it. You should get to know people first before you make a judgement based on media sound bites."

"Charity drives for clothes and used goods—you know the ones where they leave a bag at your house to be filled and then they collect it from next to your letterbox—well they've found that households in low socioeconomic areas give a bigger percentage than higher socioeconomic households."

"You can't judge all wealthy people based on a handful of personal experiences and sensationalist media reports. I'm sure there are plenty of altruistic endeavours out there."

The conversation went to and fro for a while. He was sure she wouldn't see his family in the same light as the Reids. Still, as she'd said of Jonno, hopefully she'd be too far gone when she found out.

"So, when are you heading back?" she wanted to know.

"Late tomorrow morning. I'm on a walk this week. There's a new guide starting on Monday, so I will be shadowing him, and I'll need to make sure everything's been organised."

"Will you have time to come out with me before you go?"

He raised an eyebrow at her request. "What did you have in mind?"

"Well, I got to see the Twelve Apostles at sunrise, so I thought it only fair to return the favour and see if you want to head out from Bondi on the coastal walk at sunrise."

Jacob didn't need any convincing for the chance to spend some more time with Matisse. As it was, he stretched the evening out to keep her with him as long as possible. She readily agreed to a stroll around Circular Quay after their meal, leaning her head against his shoulder from time to time as they walked. There were plenty of people around taking advantage of the mild evening, so he wasn't inclined to shower her with too much affection in public, although he was sorely tempted. He decided he would just have to be content with holding her hand and the occasional side hug.

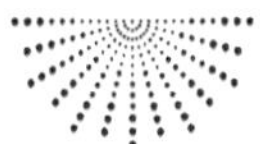

atisse had arranged to meet Jacob down at the surf club. Along with her camera on a cross-body strap, she was toting a backpack of food and a bag of camera gear which she passed off to Jacob as soon as she could. Despite the early hour there was a spring in her step. She was looking forward to showing Jacob her part of Sydney.

He was waiting at the corner of the arch-fronted Bondi Surf Bathers' Life Saving Club building that had been founded in 1907. It was too early for the Australian flag to be in position, but she looked up anyway.

~

THERE WEREN'T many people around, which suited Jacob. Much less chance to be recognised. Although a warm day was predicted, at this hour it was quite cool. The breeze was whipping up foam in the pre-dawn light.

"This is actually the first time I've done this walk since the accident. If we get to Bronte, I'll be doing well. Can't see that I'll make it all the way to Coogee Beach, though."

They set off around Queen Elizabeth Drive past the double-storey cream colonnade building of the Bondi Bathing Pavilion. Matisse told him the local council was looking at an upgrade for the building, but it was a contentious issue with the residents. As they walked, he took in the rounded white lifeguard station, a familiar sight for locals and tourists alike, having featured in the reality show, *Bondi Rescue*. Nearby, a life-size bronze statue of a lifesaver strained forward as if he was about to dive into the waves to perform a rescue.

Jacob followed Matisse. She was keen to show him the murals on the sea wall.

"The artwork is here for six months at a time," she gestured to the murals as they walked along. "A couple are permanent though." Matisse stopped in front of a painting of a young girl with a frangipani in her hair. "This is Chloe. She died in the 2002 Bali bombings in Kuta. She was fifteen." He could see she was lost in thought. Maybe remembering her own loss in Bali.

She wiped her hand across her face and started to walk again. They wandered over a grassed slope dotted with Norfolk Island pines, directly across the street from a row of shops, then up a hill to a tall, white, glass-fronted building that was home to the famous Icebergs Swim Club. The first of the year-round swimming club members were already in the larger lap pool, following the black lines up and down in the aqua water. Waves crashed over the ocean edge of the pool from time to time, briefly engulfing the swimmer in the nearest lane. The kids pool below where they were standing was currently empty for maintenance work. Matisse said with a smile that, while the adults' winter swim club was named Icebergs, the children's version was known as the Icecubes.

They both looked back towards the north. There it was—the sweeping crescent of sand that formed the iconic beach he had seen many times in photographs. Pausing to watch from a white wooden railing above the pool area, they waited.

~

THERE WAS a strip of lilac sky over Ben Buckler Point in the distance and, above it, a wide bank of fluffy clouds. The sun started to make its presence known and soon the cloud bank turned soft orange. Magical. Matisse worked her camera, despite the fact that Jacob, a mere heartbeat away from her, was causing her system to go haywire. Again.

Her companion had never travelled the coastal walk before and was taken by the wind-sculptured sandstone formations overhanging the track as they made their way down from street level.

Twenty minutes in, and Matisse knew she was going to struggle with her leg. She was in considerable pain from climbing all the steps. Making frequent stops to take photos gave her some respite, but she pushed on regardless.

Mackenzie's Point on the headland was her chosen spot to stop for coffee and a bite to eat. Breakfast, with the spectacular views north to Bondi and south towards their destination at Coogee. They found a picnic table and Matisse pulled containers out of the bag Jacob had set down.

As they sat side by side enjoying the ocean view, Matisse explained that the annual Sculpture by the Sea festival held in October had been a drawcard for about twenty years. She indicated the park behind her. "There are works of art stretching all the way from Bondi to the beach at Tamarama. There is always a heap of sculptures around the park here."

"Popular?"

"Absolutely. It's a toss-up whether it's worth the people-crush to see the artwork. But getting here early helps."

MATISSE SLIPPED her free hand into his as they walked, which he released to walk behind her when someone approached from the other direction. Jacob was impressed with the view, and while he loved being with Matisse he was concerned with her obvious physical discomfort. "Are you sure you want to keep going?"

She nodded, but he was unconvinced.

"Sorry but I'm not going to piggyback you the rest of the way." She shot him a wry grin.

MATISSE PUSHED herself to make the stairs on the ascent to Tamarama. If she could just get to the section of the walkway that swept around the beach area, they could stop for a breather. Soon enough she peeled off her jacket and sat down, grateful for a drink. Jacob had already shed his jacket as the wind started to die down and the sun warmed up.

Jacob dropped his arm along her shoulder and leaned back, crossing a leg over his knee. Matisse closed her eyes. It was quiet and peaceful, and Matisse was sure she was about to drop off to sleep. She roused herself and looked sideways at her companion. "Let's go," she told him. Matisse went to stand up, but Jacob reached for her arm and tugged her back down gently.

"Let's not," he suggested, leaning closer, his breath fanning a delicious shiver down her spine. His thumb caressed her hand as he pressed light kisses near her ear.

She swallowed and pushed to her feet.

He grinned lazily and joined her reluctantly. "You seriously want to keep walking?"

She nodded. "I'll do a deal though—just until the walkway a bit further along, and then we can call it quits." She winced in pain as she started again, pulling him along with her.

Eventually they arrived at a newer section of the coastal walk which featured a fine series of timber stairs that ran in front of the Waverley cemetery. Million-dollar views for people who could never appreciate the scenery.

Matisse was relieved to reach this end point for today. To be honest, if she hadn't been in so much pain, she'd have loved nothing better than to just keep walking with Jacob and not stop. Leaning heavily on the stair rail, the throbbing pain from her leg overshadowed almost every other feeling she had. Why hadn't she thought to pack some painkillers? To try and take her mind off herself, she chatted to Jacob about some of those buried on site.

"Believe it or not, the journalist JF Archibald, the founder of the Bulletin magazine who gave his name to the art prize, is buried here at Waverley."

"Really?"

"I've checked out who else is buried here."

"Such as?"

"Well, Victor Trumper, the cricket player for one. Poets Henry Lawson and Henry Kendall. Australia's first female Olympic gold medallist was a swimmer, and she's buried here—Fanny Durack. Oh, and the only Australian survivor of the Titanic, um, what was her name? Edna ... no that wasn't it, Evelyn someone or other, I think." Matisse glanced up and stopped suddenly. "Look at that."

A tall ship under full sail was making its way up the coast and had hit a patch of silver water shimmering in the light. She pulled her camera up and took a few frames, moving around. Then turning her back to the ship, she scanned the cemetery. Jacob followed as she made her way up one of the internal roads. She walked behind a line of gravestones and lined up a shot between some of the headstones, including a white marble angel in the foreground. Jacob tucked his hand under her elbow as they walked to the meeting place for his car, pausing as she stopped to read yet another headstone.

"How was your walk?" Max asked as Matisse walked in the door, limping visibly, the expression on her face obviously concerning him. She screwed her nose up. "The company was good, the leg not so good, I'm afraid."

"Much pain?"

"Yeah, well, it could be worse I suppose. I think I'll grab something for it and hit the shower. Oh, Jacob said to say hi—he's heading back to Victoria to start a walk first thing tomorrow."

A short time later she returned to where Max was still sitting reading the paper.

"Dee still asleep?"

"You know Dee, it's a bit early for her yet."

"So, did we get a run in the paper?" she asked.

"Well, sort of."

"What's that supposed to mean?" Max opened the paper to the page in question, folded it back and handed it to her. She was quiet as she read the paper, feeling the colour drain from her face.

"Reclusive Victorian millionaire, Jacob Davis, was seen out and about at the opening of an exhibition by up-and-coming artist Matisse Reynolds at the Stanard Gallery. Davis indicated he had recently met the artist and was lending some support as she had been through a difficult time in her life." The article went on to talk about her accident.

Matisse sat down heavily and handed it back.

"He never mentioned anything," she said in barely a whisper. "I had no idea he was a ... millionaire. I know he has a lot of business interests and, well, his house is pretty impressive ... still ..." She trailed off, confused.

"I suspect he chose not to tell you. I mean, after all, when you look at it from his point of view, any time he pursues a relationship he would always have in the back of his mind whether it was about him as a person or his money."

"I guess."

As soon as she could excuse herself, Matisse took herself off to do an internet search on Jacob Davis.

There wasn't a lot of information available. Her eyes widened as she realised the extent of his business holdings and that of the Davis family. She felt intimidated.

Now that she thought about it, there were plenty of sign-posts along the way, and it made sense that last night at dinner he had been so defensive about wealthy people in general. Then there were the photos with women, at least three different ones pictured with him at various events, but they were taken a couple of years back.

There was something about the photo in today's paper that bothered her, but initially she wasn't able to put a finger on it. Then suddenly it dawned on her. Jacob had been standing next to her when the photographer had asked to take the picture, but in the photograph in the paper, he was on the other end, as if he didn't want to be associated with her for some reason.

All she could think was that she was being rejected, like the Reid family had rejected her.

CHAPTER NINETEEN

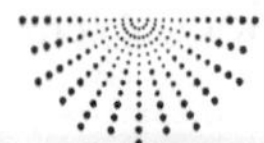

*L*eaning forward on his elbows, Jacob dropped his head into his hands. He couldn't get Matisse's ashen face out of his mind. She had successfully avoided him for days, and when he finally managed to catch up with her it hadn't gone well.

Most of what she talked about must have made sense to her mind, but not to his. The upshot of it was, the last time she had fallen in love with someone from a wealthy background it had all ended badly, and she refused to go down that track again.

He shook his head. Usually, women were falling over themselves to be by his side as soon as they found out about his money. Now that he'd finally found someone who he thought liked him for himself, she couldn't back away fast enough when she discovered his wealth.

He'd tried and failed to convince her that the Davis and Reid families were poles apart. His family all loved her, and there was no talk of her being after his money. Okay, apart from Todd that time. He'd worried that his younger brother may have said something untoward to Matisse, but after confronting his sibling he was sure that wasn't the case. Todd was just having a go at him because he could—it had never gone any further.

Jacob had planned to tell her exactly how he felt about her, but in the end, he took a deep breath and respected her wishes and backed off to give her some space—the very last thing he wanted to be doing.

~

MATISSE WAS grateful to escape to Sydney for Christmas with Max and Dee. Mel had invited her to spend Christmas with the extended Davis family—cousins, aunts and uncles—which would run to about forty people. Wall-to-wall Davis family was too much to cope with in her fragile state. Okay, honestly, it was just Jacob.

She was able to use the excuse that she was the only real family Max and Dee had, which was true up to a point. While Mel accepted her explanation, she knew her friend had picked up on her change of demeanour after the exhibition in Sydney. To be honest, she was avoiding Mel too.

Although Max and Dee were pleased to see her over Christmas, she knew they were concerned she was on her own. She made no mention of Jacob, and if asked gave some vague response and changed the subject.

At the lunch they hosted for various strays who otherwise had no one to celebrate the Christmas season with, Matisse struggled, trying to put on an appropriate festive facade. Sitting around the table with the others she pulled on the offered bonbon and stuck the paper crown on her head along with the other guests. Laden platters were passed around but there was only a small amount of food on her plate. No appetite. The slips of paper with jokes were read out with much hilarity, but her smiles were forced.

Their visitors may not have picked up on her internal turmoil, but Max and Dee knew. She had come so far in the last few months, learning to live again. But now she was on the edge of a dark place. Again.

~

THE MISERABLE WET weather that had enveloped the Cape over the last couple of weeks matched his mood. Jake had thrown the gossip magazines on his office desk in disgust after reading them. They never let the facts get in the way of their stories, and he'd unwittingly given them plenty of material to work with. He was usually so careful to avoid public scrutiny but maybe being around Matisse had clouded his judgment.

He had grabbed the magazines with a pile of papers at the airport on his way through, hoping that the attendant wouldn't recognise his photo on the covers, grateful at least they weren't the lead photos. It was late and the teenage girl on the register was obviously tired and bored, checking the time on her wristwatch as she rang up the amounts and handed him the change.

The magazines had come out within days of each other, each with totally different stories.

"*Speculation is mounting that the bachelor days of Victorian millionaire businessman Jacob Davis may be coming to an end with recent reports he has been spotted squiring Sydney artist Matisse Reynolds around in recent weeks, both in his hometown and hers. A spokesman said they met when Reynolds moved into the Cape Otway district following her recovery from a motorbike accident in Bali two years ago. Davis was amongst a crowd of supporters at the opening of her latest exhibition at the Stanard Gallery, and was later rumoured to have had a private tour of the Archibald Prize display with the up-and-coming artist. Davis reportedly introduced her as his girlfriend to a group of trekkers on a recent Great Ocean Road walk he was leading. An eyewitness said they couldn't keep their hands off each other.*" At least the accompanying phone photo was blurry.

Then there was the headline "*Millionaire businessman caught cheating on artist girlfriend*". The photo was of him supposedly cosying up to an older woman at a tourism awards function in Singapore. The fact that her husband was sitting on the other side of her, conveniently cropped out of the picture, as Jacob leaned down to hear something she was saying, wasn't mentioned.

The worst of the tabloids was the one that maintained he had a secret family. A son and daughter, with twins on the way —which of course was attributed to the couple he and Matisse had met on the beach while minding Ashton and Lily.

A late-night phone call from Max alerted him to her already precarious state of mind. Jacob was concerned this media circus might tip Matisse back over the edge. What must she be thinking? Desperate to contact her and make amends, he drove into Apollo Bay.

His sister had a few choice words to say. Mel had warned him his actions could come back to bite him, but the extent of it had shocked even her. "What were you thinking?" she admonished him as he tried to explain the mess. "It's not me you should be telling, it's Matisse."

"I would, if I knew where she was. You wouldn't know by any chance?" As soon as Mel hesitated, he knew the answer. "Mel?"

"Yes, I know where she is, but she asked me not to tell anyone, especially you. She needed to get away and think."

"The cabin is all closed up."

"She's not renewing the lease. She's intending to go back to Sydney."

Jacob swore as he ran his fingers through his hair in frustration. "I need to talk to her."

"She'll be back in a few days; you can talk to her then. In the meantime, you need to do some explaining to our parents. They're none too impressed by the media reports."

He winced. "Of course they're not."

THE WET WEATHER CONTINUED. The Bureau of Meteorology

was calling it a significant rain event, which meant widespread flooding in the Otway area. There were already landslips in several spots along the Great Ocean Road, blocking vehicular access. Heavy rain in the catchment area meant local creeks and rivers were rising everywhere.

Jacob paced the floor. He knew the water level in the creek was bound to reach the cabin. There wasn't much time left. He was compelled to go down there, even though he knew she wasn't there, wanting to get her gear out, and her artwork, before it was too late.

The first thing he did was check the water level. It was rising rapidly—almost to the point of breaking its banks. He knew he would have to move fast. He hauled her bench seat from the water's edge up to the ute and threw it into the back tray, then manoeuvred the Ranger right up to the cabin steps, cursing himself for forgetting the spare key. The door splintered as he kicked it repeatedly to gain access and hurried to the pile of canvases in the back corner. Moving quickly, he snatched them up and shoved them into plastic garbage bags that he hoped would protect them enough before taking them out to the car. Thankfully, the rain had eased slightly.

The stack of canvases against the wall steadily got smaller. Many were still blank, some were not. There wasn't time to take them in—except for one. It was at the back, and covered. He picked up the painting, and as he swung it up, the material fell to the floor. Bending to retrieve it he caught sight of the portrait and stopped in his tracks. He was the subject. It was unfinished, but unmistakably himself.

There was a piece of paper on the floor next to it. When he picked it up, he realised it was actually a ten by fifteen photo that she must have used as a reference. The quality of her artwork momentarily stunned him, but he didn't have time to stand around.

With the water rapidly reaching the back steps of the cabin, Jacob moved on to the paint supplies and other bits and pieces, almost running back and forth to his four-wheel drive. Thankfully, everything was neat and tidy, making it faster to clear out.

The back seat was soon filled with a couple of suitcases and bedding. Grabbing several boxes at once he tripped as he hurried, sending the top box flying. Sidestepping the mess, he practically threw the cartons into the car and came back to retrieve what he'd dropped.

A pile of photos had fallen out of a large envelope. He scooped them up and paused. It was Matisse with a male who had to be Jonno. He could just make out the surf pendant in the opening of Jonno's shirt. They were both laughing at the camera. Unable to help himself, he shuffled the pile. If there was any doubt about the way Matisse felt about Jonno, it was clearly evident in the photos that they were deeply in love.

What he wouldn't give for her to look that way at him. A sudden pain knifed him in the gut. Clenching his jaw, he shoved the jealousy down quickly, along with the photos back into the envelope, and pushed it into the side of the nearest box in the car. The water was starting to lap at the bottom cabin step as he drove away.

MATISSE SURVEYED the rain-sodden landscape for the umpteenth time. She had been holed up for a couple of weeks. It had been raining for much of that, not that it worried her. More inconvenient than anything. Paint, along with everything else, took so much longer to dry in the damp weather.

Damp—that was a joke. She couldn't believe how much rain had fallen since she had been here. The numerous small canvases she had taken with her had long been finished, but thankfully their completion had allowed her to take a couple of steps back from the dark edge she had found herself on such a short time ago. Her painting had once again worked its soothing power on her.

Cabin fever had set in, though, and she was more than a little anxious to be out and on the road. The isolation of this spot had been welcome—although being away from others, from Jacob and his family, hadn't given her as much peace of mind and clarity going forward as she had hoped. Sure, she seemed to get on well with them, but that was before she knew what she knew now.

In her mind, she went over and over every interaction she'd had with the Davis family. Trying to analyse them, looking for a sign that they hadn't ever approved of her hanging out with Jacob. They seemed nice, regular, salt-of-the-earth type people, and accepted her at their family get-togethers.

But she didn't belong in their world. She was just an artist who happened to be able to make a decent living doing what she loved most. It wasn't a "real job". Jacob's business world was way out of her comfort zone—way out of her league. He would be much better off without her. He needed someone more glamorous to be at his side when he attended social functions, not some awkward little artist.

Then there were those magazine articles. She wished she had never seen them. Jacob shouldn't have made that comment about having twins—obviously the older couple on the beach that day had figured out who he was, and who knows how much money they got for that juicy titbit? She didn't regret helping him out mid-walk when he had trouble with that divorced woman. Matisse was as much to blame for that story as he was. But the Singapore one? Mel had told her to hear Jacob out before she jumped to any conclusions, and she guessed she should give him the benefit of the doubt based on the other articles. Everything wasn't always as it seemed.

Mel had been adamant in her belief that Matisse should have it out with her brother. Matisse was just as stubborn in her reluctance. By rights, she knew she should talk to him, but wasn't sure if she was brave enough to do it face-to-face. Maybe she could just sneak back to Sydney and try to forget about him.

Who was she kidding? That was never going to happen. Jacob had coaxed her back into life and living, and, more importantly, feeling deeply again.

Matisse *was* grateful. Maybe she could ... write a letter of thanks when she was safely back in Sydney.

~

CONDITIONS WEREN'T ideal to head back, but she was low on supplies both of the food and the artistic kind. Matisse rang Mel to let her know she was planning to return, but had to be content with leaving a message on the answering machine.

She turned her attention to the road. The trip was tedious and slow going. The van probably wasn't the right sort of vehicle to use in this weather—a big four-wheel drive like Jake's would have been better, but what she had was the van. Matisse pushed on regardless.

The window was open to try to clear some of the windscreen fog. The rain had slowed to a light drizzle. Matisse slowed the van to a halt at the crossing over Johnson Creek, and got out to survey the depth of the water. She checked the flood marker posts. The water level hardly registered. It wasn't flowing very fast, so after some deliberation she figured she would be okay to go ahead.

Climbing back into the driver's seat, she put the car into gear and started across. About halfway, the engine stalled. She tried to restart it to no avail. A wave of water swept through and the van started to move sideways.

"If it's flooded, forget it."

The words of the government advertising campaign mocked her.

She remembered.

Too late.

Water quickly started filling the cabin and she knew she needed to get out. There wasn't much time. With shaking hands,

Matisse grabbed the top of the door frame, closed her eyes and tried to suck in a calming breath as she struggled to hoist herself out the window. She managed to get one foot onto the window edge, and with the other she used the side mirror as a step. One wrong move and she would fall into the churning brown water below.

Desperate, she clambered up and dragged herself onto the roof, sprawling on her stomach and hanging on for dear life as the van jerked crazily under the force of the water.

She closed her eyes, dizzy and nauseous as she bucked and swayed around as though she was on some demented fair ride. Amazingly, the van got caught up against a tree. There was only one thing she could do. Shaking, she pulled herself onto her knees, took a deep breath and stretched out towards a branch, willing her arm to stretch that little bit further, terrified she would overbalance and fall off. Somehow, she was able to grab hold and pull herself across and into a tree fork just as the car was washed away.

Matisse wedged herself in the tree, wrapped her arms around the branch, and clung on as the brown swirling water rose higher, carrying all manner of debris with it on its thundering way downstream.

CHAPTER TWENTY

Once home, Jacob had barely hauled the gear out when he heard the phone ring. He took the stairs three at a time and grabbed the handset.

Mel didn't beat around the bush. "Jacob, I'm worried about Matisse."

"Why? What's wrong?"

"She went up to Carlisle and was due back today. She left me a message to say she was on her way. I rang to tell her not to go via Johnson Creek, but there was no answer. She must've already left. Jacob, she should have been back by now." Jacob could hear the concern in her voice and tried to stay calm, even though he felt his stomach drop.

He sucked in a shuddering breath and swallowed hard before answering. "Okay, I'll take a drive out that way and I'll get Todd to come with me. Is Adam around?" His brother-in-law had been run off his feet along with the rest of the State Emergency Service crews in the area.

Jacob's helicopter crews had already been pressed into assisting and he expected a call anytime soon for his own chopper to join them.

"He's heading out now, he'll meet you at the turnoff."

Jacob hung up and sprang into action, calling out for Todd on his way down the stairs.

Todd came to the door of his room in just a pair of boxer shorts. "What's up, man?"

"I need your help. Mel rang and said Matisse was due back from Carlisle and hasn't turned up. She wouldn't know about the danger of Johnson Creek." Todd took a while to process the information. "I need you, c'mon mate."

Todd swore. "Are you going to fly in?"

Jacob shook his head. "Visibility around there isn't good enough, and there won't be anywhere to land. Far too dangerous."

Todd disappeared to throw on some clothes. With his boots in one hand, he ran to the garage, grabbed a Driza-Bone off a hook on his way past and jumped in beside his brother as the Ranger roared out.

"Jeez, calm down, mate," Todd told Jacob as he lurched around while trying to pull on his boots. "You're not going to be any help if you slide us off the road." Todd eyed his brother as Jacob hung on grimly, white knuckles on the steering wheel, his mouth set in a hard line.

Jake arrived at the meeting place ahead of his brother-in-law. He killed the engine but was too worked up to sit in the car and just wait. The rain wasn't bothering him as he paced up and down next to the four-wheel drive, praying that nothing had happened to Matisse. He didn't know what he would do if ... desperate to rein in his thoughts he was relieved when Adam pulled up alongside less than ten minutes later. They spoke briefly before continuing on their way.

The rain got heavier, obscuring his vision as he switched the wipers to flat out. It took all his concentration to keep the vehicle on the road.

~

As soon as they got to the creek crossing, he was out of the car scanning the surroundings. Adam joined him, still wearing his orange SES uniform, and tipped his cap back as they surveyed the swollen creek before them. The angry brown water surged past, carrying tree branches and other debris on its way downstream. Maybe she'd turned back and hadn't tried to cross the flooded creek. Maybe he was wasting his time. Maybe ...

"Oh, dear God, no!"

He'd spotted the back end of a van sticking up out of the water forty metres or so downstream. He scrambled down the embankment and ran along just above the water level, slipping every few metres. Suddenly he stopped. Adam, right behind him, nearly knocked him off his feet.

"That's her van, I'm sure of it." The realisation that Matisse had probably drowned hit him like the proverbial ton of bricks. Doubling over in pain, hands on knees trying to stop them from giving way, he struggled for air. He went numb all over and couldn't form a coherent thought. His brain was screaming *No, No, No!* as his vision darkened ...

Adam belted him on the shoulder. "Look over there to the right, about one o'clock, in the trees."

Jake followed his brother-in-law's outstretched arm. There was a flash of movement. "I think that's her, Adam."

The sense of relief nearly overwhelmed him, along with the realisation that she was still in trouble. Adam wanted to wait for backup, but Jacob knew everyone was already stretched to the limit and they were short on time. Racing back to the Ranger, Jacob moved it into a better position. Adam grabbed some chains and ran them around the back of the Ranger and then around a nearby tree, and secured them. They would have to move quickly, improvising with what they had. Todd was pressed into service as they set up a makeshift rope system using the winch on the front of the Ranger. Adam prepared to enter the water, but Jake stopped him.

"I have to do this," Jake told his brother-in-law.

"Are you sure? It's been a while since you've done anything like this."

"Yes, I'm sure. You know I've done the training as well. It has to pay off sometime, Adam. Might as well be now. I'm going in."

He pulled on the black wetsuit with the distinctive orange sleeves. Luckily, he and Adam were a similar build. The rescue jacket was next. Fumbling with the straps, he cursed as he tried to adjust it for a better fit. After checking the jacket to his satisfaction, Adam handed him the matching yellow helmet and attached the harness. Walking along the sodden bank together, they strategised, as they searched for a likely entry point further upstream. Double-checking the ropes, Adam finally cleared him to go.

ONCE IN THE WATER, everything became a bit of a blur. All he could do was focus on getting to Matisse. *Hang on Matisse, I'm coming.* He fought his way down and across to the far side. The actual distance wasn't so great, but fighting against the raging water took all his strength. He was pushed under a few times, then slammed into a tree on the far bank. He grabbed a hold to work his way from one tree to the next until he reached the place where she was clinging. He could barely hear Adam over the rush of the creek. He struggled to gain a foothold, slipped and smashed his shins. Jake refocused and went again.

Eventually, he was able to haul himself into the tree beside her. She barely registered his presence as he attempted to coax her into the life jacket. It was no small wonder she was terrified. Jake tried to reassure her as he lashed them together.

"Adam and Todd are on the other side. They'll help winch us back across. Okay?" There was no response. "We have to get into the water though. We'll get taken downstream at first. You need to trust us. You need to trust me, Matisse." He put a hand under her chin and forced her to look up at him. "Do you understand?" She nodded at him mutely.

He prised her arms from the tree branch and pulled her in tight against him, wrapping one arm around her as he signalled Adam. "Okay, here we go. Hang on."

Her grip tightened around him as he pulled them out of the tree, dropping into the water. Adam and Todd worked tirelessly to bring them to safety, dragging them back through the torrent of water. Once Jacob's feet hit solid ground, he unclipped them and helped her claw her way up the bank. Thankfully she had only lost her shoes and no other clothes. Jake managed to pull the rescue jacket off her before she slipped and lay on the ground totally exhausted.

Jake fell down next to her on his hands and knees, gasping for breath, his muscles screaming at the toll the crossing had taken on his body. He could hear Matisse throwing up. Adam bent down next to her, talking in a low reassuring voice. Jake rolled onto his back and covered his face with an arm. They lay like that for a long time, too physically spent to even think about moving.

Adam eventually packed the gear away, then hauled Jacob to his feet, and between the two of them they managed to get Matisse to the Ranger. Todd was standing there awkwardly. Jake, unsteady on his feet, went and pulled the keys out of the ignition and tossed them at his younger brother. "You're up," Jacob told him.

"Seriously? You're going to let me drive?"

"Don't have much choice. Just take it easy." Jacob turned his attention back to Matisse. Taking a thick grey blanket from Adam he wrapped her into it before helping her into the car. Grabbing himself a second blanket, he slid across to where she was sitting and put his arm around her, holding her up against his chest.

"You're okay now, Matisse," he told her. "You gave me one

hell of a scare." He stroked her hair and kissed the top of her bedraggled head.

≈

MATISSE WAS TOO numb from the trauma to say anything. She was vaguely aware of Jacob's comforting arm around her, but she lost track of time. *It's okay, I'm safe, Jacob saved me.* The words spun around in her head over and over. The Ranger slipped and slid most of the way back to the main road. Matisse clutched at Jacob, who swore a couple of times as they were tossed around in the back.

≈

JACOB HELPED Matisse climb the stairs. He would have carried her if he still had any strength in his arms. But he was spent.

He steered Matisse in the direction of the master bedroom ensuite. "There's a bathrobe hanging behind the door. Will you be able to manage?" There was a slight nod as she closed the door behind her. Jacob grabbed some clothes from his walk-in robe before hitting the shower down the hall.

By the time he emerged, Adam had already arranged for the doctor to come out to the house. He'd also rung Mel to fill her in, and she promised to drive out as soon as she could. Todd had found Matisse's large black suitcase down where her gear had been left in the garage, and hauled it upstairs so she had some dry clothes to wear.

≈

MATISSE WAS STILL in a daze when she wandered out to the kitchen. The small part of her brain that was still functioning noticed the snug-fitting long-sleeved t-shirt on her rescuer and the grey sweatpants that seemed to make his legs go on forever.

She knew she was a dishevelled sight. But there was nothing she could do about it at the moment—there was no strength in her arms to make herself more presentable. Matisse needed company. Maybe some distraction, so she wouldn't give way to the emotion that was swirling around in her brain. Snatches of her rescue were on a continuous loop.

The boys were talking at the table, their voices muffled from the water in her ears. Totally exhausted, she fixed her eyes on one of the chairs, hoping to shuffle over and sit down before she collapsed in a heap.

Her eyes were red and puffy, either from the water or crying or both, and she had made some attempt to pull her hair into line. Todd jumped up and pulled out a chair for her to join Jake who was already drinking a strong coffee, his hands wrapped firmly around the largest mug he had in his cupboard. Adam made Matisse a hot, very sweet tea, which she sipped absently. Adam sat down opposite keeping a close eye on both of them.

"Mel tried to call and tell you not to come back via Johnson Creek but you had already left," Adam told her. "We hoped you had decided to turn back."

Matisse finally found her voice. It was husky and barely a whisper. "I did stop and check it out. At that point, the water level looked okay, so I decided to go ahead. The van stalled partway across and I couldn't get it started. Then suddenly it started to move sideways. The water rose really quickly in the space of a couple of minutes. I wished I'd remembered all the 'flooded, forget it' slogans a little earlier. The cabin started to fill with water, and I had to try and get out. Luckily, I had wound the window down earlier. To be honest I have no idea how I managed to get up and onto the roof. The van crashed into a tree and I was able to grab a branch and pull myself over."

JACOB EXCHANGED glances with the other two men.

Adam leaned over to take her arms and check out her cuts and scrapes. "We'll see about getting your van out of the water when the level goes down. I don't imagine much will be salvageable." He went on in a quiet soothing voice, "The doctor will be here in about an hour. Would you like to lie down for a bit?"

"No, not really." Resting her head on folded arms down on the tabletop, she closed her eyes.

Jacob couldn't muster up the energy to close the distance between them and comfort her.

JACOB SAT in a state of disbelief talking quietly with Adam and Todd as each tried to process their own thoughts.

The doctor emerged from the master bedroom. "She's a very lucky young lady," he told them. "I've given her a tetanus shot. Here are some antibiotics. Make sure she takes them, and I've given her a sedative as well."

He looked over at her rescuer. "Jake. I'd like to check you out."

"I'm fine, Doc—really."

"Nonetheless, I'd feel better if I did."

"I appreciate you coming out, Martin," Jake told the doctor as he pulled his shirt back on a short time later. "I'm a bit concerned the media would have a field day with it if they found out, and it's the last thing either of us needs."

CHAPTER TWENTY-ONE

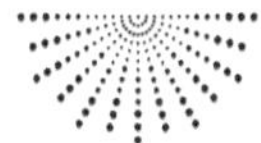

*J*ake had no idea how long he'd been sitting, elbows propped up on the table, head in hands, when his sister put a comforting hand on his shoulder.

"Hey Jake, are you okay?" The silence that followed echoed in the room.

He looked up at the wall opposite the table and tried to pull his brain out of the fog that had gradually enveloped him over the course of the day. He was so very weary.

"I was sure I'd lost her, Mel," his voice croaked. "It was the worst feeling ever. Absolute, pure agony. It was a miracle she managed to get out of the van and into the tree ... And to hang on long enough ... I still don't know how I managed to get her to solid ground."

"You love her a lot, don't you?" she asked, rubbing her hand across his shoulders.

He nodded. "More than she knows."

"So ... are you going to tell her anytime soon?"

"I thought she got the general idea, but Jonno is still in the equation there somewhere. I still think she's afraid of making a commitment, of falling in love in case it all goes awry like it did with Jonno ... oh, and she's gotten it into her head that the Davis family can't possibly accept her ..."

"Well you need to convince her otherwise, Jake. You know we all love her."

"I'm not sure that I can. Lord knows, I've tried. Jonno's family has a lot to answer for. I still can't believe they would make a judgement without actually meeting her in person."

"Guess she didn't fit in with their plans and expectations for his future. Maybe it was easier to disapprove of someone they'd never met, in case she challenged the status quo. Their loss."

He nodded in agreement. "I just don't know where I stand."

"Well, I'm here for as long as needed. Andi took the kids over to Mum and Dad's."

"Thanks."

When Matisse finally woke up, she had no idea where she was. Glancing around the unfamiliar room, she saw Mel curled up in a large chair by the bed and wondered how long she had been there. As her head cleared, the memories of yesterday came flooding back, literally. She tried to move gingerly under the covers; sore, but not as bad as she knew she would be tomorrow.

"Good morning, Matisse, how did you sleep?" Mel stretched and grabbed a couple of pillows and put them behind her friend to prop her up.

"Um, oh, I don't know. So, so, I guess."

"I hear you gave the boys a bit of a scare yesterday."

"Not as big as the one I gave myself."

"I wouldn't bet on it, Matisse. Jacob was positive you were still in the van. He'd practically convinced himself you had drowned. He was distraught. Then all the drama of getting you out of the tree and back across the creek took a huge toll on him. He's still a bit of a mess, to be honest."

Matisse was horrified she had caused so much trouble for

Jake and the others. She closed her eyes and sank back into the pillows. Reliving the nightmare again. She swallowed hard and tried to banish the images.

"Jacob cares for you ... an awful lot ... our whole family does, Matisse." Mel hesitated then went on, "Do you feel the same way?"

As her hand fluttered to the bed covers, Matisse fidgeted with the seams on the edge. Sure, she cared for Jacob. Cared for all of them, but ... her head nodded of its own accord.

"Don't you think it's time to let him know?"

"I guess."

"Matisse, he thinks you can't love him because of what happened with Jonno."

Matisse couldn't stop the tears welling up in her eyes as she looked at her friend. "I want to, Mel, but I don't know if I can."

"Can you at least give it some serious thought? He needs to know one way or another. The not-knowing is killing him. I've never seen him in such a state. Ever. Please don't leave him hanging like this." Mel leaned over the bed and gave her friend a kiss on the cheek and changed the subject. "Would you like something to eat?"

SHE HADN'T SEEN JACOB. Had no idea where he was. Couldn't catch any sound of his voice.

His bed was huge. Matisse felt dwarfed by its sheer size and luxury, and she could smell his scent—especially in the pillows. It gave her some sense of comfort, although she would prefer the man himself. She wished she wasn't in the bed alone, that he was with her, holding her close. That she could wake up next to him in the mornings and snuggle into him.

Matisse was restless. She tossed and turned for most of the night, her mind a jumble of thoughts. In the end, at first light she knew what she needed to do. Rummaging around in the suitcase Todd had left by the door, she pulled on a pair of jeans and a jacket over a long-sleeve shirt. Jamming her feet into old canvas slip-ons, she let herself out of the house as quietly as she could, with Charlie shadowing her every move.

In the half light of pre-dawn she was able to find her way to the path that led down to the beach. Gripping the rail, she stepped carefully down the wooden steps one at a time until she reached the bottom. Sitting on the edge, she pulled off her shoes and tossed them next to her on the last step then eased off until she could drop down. The sand was cold, the water even colder, but no matter, it was time.

JACOB HAD BEEN WALKING for most of the night when he found himself down on the beach below his house. After the flood, he realised just how much Matisse meant to him. He loved her and couldn't imagine a life without her by his side, but he had no idea how she really felt about him. His sigh was carried away on the cool breeze. Suddenly Charlie came bounding around the corner and cannoned into him.

"Hey Charlie, where did you come from?" He stooped down to pat his dog, then realised Matisse might be nearby. He stood up.

"Where is she, boy? Where's Matisse?" Charlie shot off.

Jake spotted her with the bottom of her pants rolled up, in water almost to her knees, but he somehow knew he didn't need to be concerned. Her hair was loose, blowing all over the place. He was hidden from view by a rock formation, but close enough to see. He grabbed Charlie's collar before the canine gave him away.

MATISSE PULLED her hair back and fumbled as she unclipped

the necklace and held it up in front of her, watching the medallion as it spun around. "I miss you, Jonno. Part of me will always love you, but I need to move on with my life. Goodbye, sweetheart."

~

HE SAW her kiss the medallion, then close it up in her hand and throw it as far as she could. As soon as it hit the water, she turned and waded out.

Even though he hadn't heard her words, Jacob realised the significance of what she had just done, and his heart filled with hope.

~

CHARLIE RAN UP TO HER. "Where have you been, boy?" she scolded him.

"With me, actually," Jacob told her. She looked up, startled, trying to process that Jacob was beside her. He looked tired but oh-so-good in the tight blue jeans he was wearing and the white t-shirt that peeked out from under the partially-zipped brown bomber jacket. His hair was messy, as if he'd been running his fingers through it over and over. She wanted to fling herself at him and hold him tight. She was indebted to him for saving her life. But it was so much more than that.

"Couldn't sleep?" he said.

"Ah, no."

"How are you going?"

"Um, okay, I guess. Pretty battered and bruised ... you?"

"Yeah same." He went on, "The cabin got washed off its stumps, did you know?"

"Yeah, Mel said. Is anything salvageable?"

"Not sure yet. It's still in one piece, sort of, just not where it should be. Won't know until I can get in there for a closer look.

We might be able to reposition it. At least I hope so. There's a lot of memories down there."

There was an awkward pause before Matisse thought how to fill it.

"Mel mentioned you managed to get my gear out. I'm very grateful."

"That's okay. There's some pretty amazing work there, Matisse."

"Ah, thanks."

"There's one particular portrait I'm curious about."

"Oh?" There were a couple of recent ones she had been working on, but she suspected she knew which one he was talking about.

"Where did you get the photo? I don't recall seeing it."

He was standing about a metre away. Neither of them moved.

"Um ... well, I didn't give you all the photos I took that day." She could feel him looking at her, she knew there was something else he wanted to say.

There was a long pause before he continued. "When I carried your gear out, I dropped one of the boxes and some photos fell out ... from Bali ... you and Jonno looked very happy ... very in love." He didn't know why he was torturing himself, but he had to find out once and for all.

She had been studying the sand on her feet, then she looked up at him. Time stood still. He wasn't quite able to comprehend all the emotions that flitted across her face. He wasn't sure he could comprehend his own emotions for that matter.

"Yes, he was the love of my life," she paused, "past tense." Matisse trailed off and glanced up the beach biting her lip. Taking a deep breath, she went on. "But now ... unbelievably ... it's you." It was barely a whisper, but it was there.

He let the words wash over him. It was what he'd been waiting to hear, and he just wanted to sweep her up into his arms, but he sensed there was more she needed to say.

"Jacob, you've saved my life, in more ways than one. You've saved me from … fading away. I never believed I would be able to be truly happy again, and to find love a second time … I can't begin to fathom that I've been able to find someone else I want to spend my life with." She put her hand up to his cheek and he covered it with his own hand. Turning her palm over, he planted a tender kiss. She shivered but he didn't think it was because of the cool breeze.

"Jacob Davis, I need you to know I love you."

He pulled her into his arms and kissed her gently. "I love you," he told her, his voice thick with emotion. There were still words that needed to be said. Conversations. They could wait for now. His lips claimed hers as the dawn broke.

Charlie snuffled around their legs. They ignored him as they gave themselves up to the embrace.

EPILOGUE

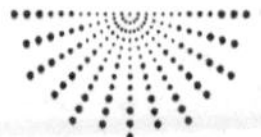

*J*acob rolled over in bed and reached his arm out, but the space beside him was empty. Not that he was surprised. He knew exactly where she would be. Despite having the new art studio attached to the main house, with stunning ocean views that she absolutely adored, Matisse still enjoyed getting back to the cabin. After all, it was where they'd first met.

Following the flood, it had been rebuilt, further back from the creek and elevated, hopefully to avoid damage next time there was a deluge. It wasn't quite as spartan anymore. He'd had power connected. There was a decent compact kitchen and bathroom. Sometimes she just needed to clear her head. They often escaped for a long weekend. To her it was perfect for painting and lovemaking. Or so she said. He reached to the floor and grabbed his jeans from where he'd dropped them the night before and pulled on a shirt, rolling the sleeves as he padded out to where she was working. Charlie was stretched out on the floormat by the back door, snoozing.

~

THE LARGE COLOURFUL canvas propped up against the side wall couldn't help but draw his attention. He grinned. Yesterday, Matisse had finally convinced him to paint with her. He wasn't sure why he'd agreed, but if he'd known how things would end up, he would have relented a long time ago.

She had called him over to the canvas before he'd even finished dressing. He should have seen the imp of mischief gleam in her eye, but to be honest, he'd been so distracted by the old white knit jumper that had slid deliciously off her shoulder that he hadn't noticed. Before he knew it, he'd had hold of a paintbrush full of colour and was dragging it across the canvas alongside her own brush strokes. He had followed her lead, not sure what she had in mind for this piece of artwork as they worked side by side. Surprisingly he found it ... not cathartic exactly, but relaxing in a way he didn't expect.

In his peripheral vision he had noticed Matisse paint her fingers and add some quick daubs to the centre of the work and repeat the process a couple more times. Then she had said his name, and as he turned it happened. Her palm had slapped against his bare chest. Fingerprints. Over his heart actually. How cute ... and poetic. Retaliating, he had daubed her nose and cheek with the brush he was holding. Cradling his cheek, more paint, she went in for a kiss. Dropping the brush Jacob had caught her around the waist and pulled her in closer ... and tickled her. It was on.

He loved the sound of her laughter joining his as they had tussled lightheartedly. Inevitably he had slipped, pulling her down to the floor on top of him in a tangle of denim-clad legs, arms and ... lips ...

~

"SORRY, DID I WAKE YOU?" She didn't turn to look at him.

"No, not at all." He stood watching her paint, one bare foot tucked behind the other. Her hair was pulled into a high ponytail that swung as she tipped her head to one side for a minute, then reached out to brush on more paint. The apron she normally wore was still on its peg nearby. If he waited long enough, he knew his old Geelong Cats AFL sweatshirt would ride up enough to give him a tantalising glimpse, probably of the satin and lace underwear she normally wore. He could easily stand there all day watching her create. After a few minutes, she stepped back.

"I think it's done."

He walked over and slipped his arms around his wife. She leaned back, relaxing against his chest as he kissed her neck and wrapped his arms firmly around her upper body. Her paint-splattered hand reached back to his cheek. He kissed it as well.

Jacob knew this particular painting well by now. The silhouettes. They started light, with the colours of Bali, then thick heavy blackness for a long time. Gradually, silhouette by silhouette, the light started to appear again. The final silhouette was almost all colour, typical of the Cape area, but there was still a touch of darkness shadowing the outline.

"I don't know if I will ever quite get rid of the darkness, but I think I've come such a long way."

She turned in his arms as he rested his forehead on the top of her head.

"Thank you," she said simply, and drew him down for a kiss.

THE END

ABOUT THE AUTHOR

As a teenager, Alison Joy wrote stories in her head at night before she fell asleep. She still does, but finally decided to get some of the stories out of her head and onto paper, then computer, and finally published. She enjoys being able to say what goes on in her characters' lives, who falls in love with whom, unexpected journeys, and changing things if she doesn't like it.

A long-term resident of Queensland's capital city, Brisbane, she is a recent convert to e-reading. Nothing will beat a physical book, of course, but for storage practicalities—especially when travelling—the e-reader rules.

As well as reading, she also enjoys photography and is a procraftinator from way back.

alisonjoywriter.com

 instagram.com/itsa.joy